My name is Darcy. I see the extraordinary in the everyday and the wonder in the world around me.

I find the tangerine from earlier in my pocket and start peeling it again. The peel is coming away from the flesh in a lovely winding  curl, like ribbon or a pig's tail that just keeps turning and turning. I'm trying so major hard not to tear the peel so that it comes off in one fancy impressive spiral. One that will really impress Will when he's back. Peeling is about patience and confidence . . . I guess that's what life is about too.

Peel, peel, peel. My head drifts off into a dreamy place . . .

www.randomhousechildrens.co.uk

Author and illustrator Laura Dockrill is a graduate of the BRIT School of Performing Arts and has appeared at many festival and literary events across the country, including the Edinburgh Fringe, Camp Bestival, Latitude and the Southbank Centre's Imagine Festival. Named one of the top ten literary talents by *The Times* and one of the top twenty hot faces to watch by *ELLE* magazine, she has performed her work on all of the BBC's radio channels, including Gemma Cairney's Radio 1 show, plus appearances on Huw Murray, Colin Murray and Radio 4's *Woman's Hour*. Laura was the Booktrust Online Writer in Residence for the second half of 2013 and was named as a Guardian Culture Professionals Network 'Innovator, Visionary, Pioneer' in November 2013. Laura has been a roving reporter for the Roald Dahl Funny Prize, and is on the advisory panel at the Ministry of Stories. The first *Darcy Burdock* book was shortlisted for the Waterstones Children's Book Prize 2014. She lives in south London with her bearded husband.

The *Darcy Burdock* series is Laura's first writing for children. After having her stage invaded by 50 rampaging kids during a reading of her work for adults at Camp Bestival, she decided she really enjoyed the experience and would very much like it to happen again. Laura would like to make it clear that any resemblance between herself-as-a-child and Darcy is entirely accurate.

'Everyone's falling for Laura Dockrill' – VOGUE

Sorry About Me & Darcy Burdock

by LAURA DOCKRILL

CORGI BOOKS

DARCY BURDOCK: SORRY ABOUT ME
A CORGI BOOK 978 0 552 56606 3

First published in Great Britain by Corgi Books,
an imprint of Random House Children's Publishers UK
A Random House Group Company

This edition published 2014

3 5 7 9 10 8 6 4

Typeset in 12.5/15pt Baskerville MT by Falcon Oast Graphic Art Ltd

Corgi Books are published by Random House Children's Publishers UK,
61–63 Uxbridge Road, London W5 5SA

www.**randomhousechildrens**.co.uk
www.**totallyrandombooks**.co.uk
www.**randomhouse**.co.uk

Addresses for companies within The Random House Group Limited can be found at:
www.randomhouse.co.uk/offices.htm

THE RANDOM HOUSE GROUP Limited Reg. No. 954009

A CIP catalogue record for this book is available from the British Library.

Penguin Random House is committed to a sustainable future for
our business, our readers and our planet. This book is made from
Forest Stewardship Council® certified paper.

Printed and bound in Great Britain by Clays Ltd, St Ives plc

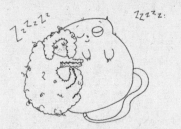

For Lois and Genie

Chapter One

Ever had one of those weeks? You know, those weeks that grown-ups talk about all the time. They say, 'It's been one of *those* weeks.' And everybody nods in deep understanding and I never knew what 'one of *those* weeks' even meant. But now I think I do.

It means a whole week where NOTHING is right. Where nothing is on your side. Where the world is like a wall, and no matter how strong you feel it just won't be knocked down. One of those weeks that makes you so mad and angry, mixed in with sad. A week so crazy that all you want is a little bit of calm. A week that makes you so cross all you want is to immediately create a recipe for a magic cake that when you take a bite of it the world zones out into relaxed calmness and nothing is difficult or hard work, and all you feel is peace.

A Peace and Quiet Cake? Does that exist? If not, I am going to invent one.

But until I do, when I'm feeling like a shaken-up bottle of lemonade mixed with an Angrosaurus rex, I do this and you can do it too.

Stand in front of the mirror. That's right. Next, open your mouth as wide as it will possibly go and roar like a lion. If your face does not change colour, then I'm afraid you are doing it wrong.

I've been feeling a lot like roaring these days. See?

ROOOOOOOOOOOOAAAAAAAAAAAAAA-RRRRRRRRRR!

Does that feel any better?

'Dinner!' Mum calls up. She is really inconsiderate, interrupting my roaring session like that – I've a good mind to tell her what's what . . . or maybe I'll just EAT HER UP instead.

The food smells incr*edible*. *Le regarde* (bit of French there for you that I learned at my new school, oh sorry about me, how I fall into wordsmith genius wordplay). See how *edible* is written secretly inside incr*edible*? In my mind the word *incredible* was made up by a big fat queen who loved pies and treats and would scream 'INCREDIBLE' every time she bit into something delicious. I hope you see her too whenever you think of using that word. It's good to use your imagination at all times rather than switching it on and off.

I let the smoky, warm and even *spicy* trail of smell lead me to the kitchen. Spicy food and me are a bit friends these days, now that I am all growed up.

'I'm becoming a vegetarian!' I announce halfway through eating my BBQ chicken wings; the sticky red sauce is all over my fingers.

Mum nods. 'Good idea,' she says. 'I've been a vegetarian.'

The idea doesn't seem quite so glamorous now

Mum's already *done* it. Why can't I be the firstest one to try *anything*?

'You don't want to be a vegetarian, Darcy, you wouldn't be able to do it. Think about all the foods from around the world that you won't get to try,' Dad says, his beard covered in the BBQ sauce so it looks like he's been snogging a pot of jam.

'I don't care. I love animals, and that's why I'm doing it. You should think about Lamb-Beth!' I scream. Lamb-Beth – my pet lamb – is in her kitchen bed, snoring and gently getting on with life.

'YOU should think about Lamb-Beth . . .' Dad shout-whispers. 'You're the one that might wake her up.'

'I'm allowed to wake her up if I want. She's *my* lamb.' I lick my fingers triumphantly and everybody goes mental at me.

'She's not JUST yours!' Poppy rages.

'She's mine too!' Hector argues.

'She belongs to EVERYBODY!' Mum snaps.

'Everybody,' Dad repeats like a squawky copy parrot; he needs to seriously consider getting some of his own material.

But alas, they are right. She is a part of the family. 'Fine,' I mumble in agreement, because if I don't agree with this they will expect ME to do EVERYTHING for her. Thank the earth I think this through otherwise that's a serious amount of lamb poo to be cleaning up.

'Darcy, if you become a vegetarian you're going to need to learn how to cook. It's nice to sometimes just eat vegetables, but on the days when we do eat meat I'm not going to cook something for you especially,' says Mum.

'*YOU* don't cook the most anyway, Dad does.' I don't know why but I want to fight with everything they are saying. I have a furious lion trapped in my bones.

'OK, whatever, just make sure you learn to cook. At least pasta.' Mum's not joining in on the battle with me today.

'YES, I WILL!' I screech. 'I can cook already anyway!'

'Yeah, if eating your bogeys counts as cooking!' Poppy snarls.

How gross – I would NEVER EVER eat my bogeys. Pick them, obviously, but eat them . . . never. Every good farmer knows not to eat his own crop.

'Go away, Poppy, you're just jealous because I've got a *thing*.'

'I've got things!' Poppy argues.

'OK, what's your *thing*?'

'Dancing.' Poppy flicks her fringe out of her eye

with her little finger so as not to get sauce in her hair.

'You gave that up.'

'All right then.' She thinks for a second. 'I've got double-jointed fingers.' She beams, wriggling her hands to try and show me. Mum looks at Poppy's sprawled-out fingers crab-walking across the table.

'That's not double-jointed, poppet,' she sighs.

'See?' I say.

'Well, fine, I'll be a vegetarian too.'

'NO!' Dad protests. 'My kids are losing their minds – everybody's going mad!'

'You can't be!' I yell. 'That's *my* thing.' Case closed, I lick the BBQ sauce off my knife.

'Darcy, don't lick your knife, and also, if you wanted to be a vegetarian for the right reasons surely you would want to convert as many people as possible? It would be great if Poppy was vegetarian with you.' Mum sips from her glass of red wine; everybody knows red wine should only be drunk out of a goblet like a king. *Hmmm*. I've lost

9

respect for Mum. Wish I was a king.

Actually, here's a full list of my current wishes:

1. That I was a grandad.
2. That I had a beard.
3. That my job was to be a customer.
4. That I had webbed fingers.
5. That I could be a writer whilst doing all of this.
6. And a mermaid, but a bit normal like marmalade, equalling a new species known as a 'mermalade'.
7. Yeah, OK, that I was a king.

'She's not even listening!' Poppy yelps, like a stupid singing canary, breaking my trail of imaginarianism. What a creaturette.

'Why doesn't everybody just calm down and stop being a smarty-pants for one single second to let me sort my head out?' I say, as if I'm one of those angry teenagers in TV programmes. I am nowhere near ready to be a teenager because if you're truly going to be a teenager, you must be committed to being livid at all times of all days. I pick at my chicken.

Dad pipes up, 'Surely you should stop eating that if you're going veggie?'

GRRR!

Mum throws Dad an evil look. 'Let her eat her food, please,' she says through gritted teeth. Mum knows that when I mean business I mean SERIOUS BUSINESS, but this chicken is too scrummy to put down just this very moment.

'Look, this is my *thing*, and so it's up to *me* to make the rules, not any of you lot. I HAVE to eat my chicken or guess what? I STARVE. Is that what you lot want? Is it? To be seeing me deaded?' I shout.

Dad laughs at the mania of me, but then Poppy starts to get upsetted. 'I just really wish right now that I had a thing!' she whines.

'You've got loads,' Mum soothes, my dramatic performance forgotten. 'You can sing, you can dance, you can act, you're funny and kind . . .'

'And annoying,' Dad jokes. 'You get that from me, obviously.'

'I know!' I crack into happiness. 'Why don't you get braces?' I know this is a bit mean because nobody as young as Poppy really wants braces, but I could see an *in* here on how to make it REALLY uncomfortable for her to eat things like toffee apples (her favouritest thing at fairs) and chewing gum – not to mention killing the enjoyment of nail biting, a most disgusting but also equally satisfying habit, EVER again. Life will be tough in braces land. 'Loads of girls have them at my school,' I add.

'NO! Poppy doesn't need braces, and they're not a fashion accessory.' Mum goes to wash her hands. I'm thinking: *Good luck getting this sticky BBQ stuff off, Mum.*

'What about glasses?' I sneer. Yeah, *ha-ha-ha-ha*, I know – I'm going to convince Poppy she needs glasses to look clever and then help her pick out some AWFUL ones, and that can be her *thing*, and my thing will be being a most glorious, healthy and hippy vegetarian who loves the planets and the bears and the lions and the rivers and the trees.

'What's wrong with you tonight?' Mum says to me.

'Nothing,' says Dad. 'She's ALWAYS like this.'

'NO, I AM NOT!' I shout. 'I *do* think Poppy should get glasses, they should be her thing.' I smile as *sweetly* as my lips can stretch. 'They are EVER so stylish. How about we do an eye test?'

'I don't want to.' Poppy shudders.

'Why not?'

'In case my eyes are terrible and then I'll need glasses.' *Great.* Reality sinks in. Poppy no longer wishes to sit snugly under my big sister wing and now wants to fly freely from the nest and as much as I want her to detour a bit and crash I know she will, as always, land on her dainty feet. Perfect Princess Poppy-ton with a cherry on her head with her big mahoosive annoying moose beast sister lagging behind. That's me. The wretched one. Plan busted.

'You won't need them. Don't be silly,' Dad reassures her. 'Come on, let's do an eye test and you can see how good you can see. It'll be fun.' He jumps up and starts looking around for bits and pieces to make his test come to life. 'OK, I'll tack this newspaper article to the wall and then I'll point to sentences and you have to read them from where you are sitting now.'

Obviously it would be way too much to ask in this house that there's some Blu-tack to hand, so Dad makes do with the bit of sellotape used to keep the plastic back of the remote control on. I leap up

14

to get a glass of milk – am not sure if vegetarians are allowed milk or not because it comes from a cow's boobie but I sink it in one glug anyway (P.S. really sorry if I just burst a blissful bubble that you were living in where milk is like snow juice or whatever . . . it's not . . . it's cow boobie juice). Being a vegetarian is actually going to be tricky. What else am I meant to eat with my Coco Pops? This eye-test thing is already looking boring and I suddenly immensely regret the whole suggestion. I could be

actually using this time to radiate my radical mind someplace else. Sigh.

Dad takes a strand of rawed spaghetti from the jar to use as the pointer. 'OK, Poppy, have a go at reading this headline here,' he says,

 using the spaghetti as his bossy stick.

'OK,' she sniffs and reads: 'BREAKING NEWS, MAN ARRESTED FOR BANK ROBBERY.'

'Perfect,' says Dad. 'And this line here, this is harder because the words are smaller . . .'

'Arnold Moose was arrested yesterday afternoon after neighbours reported him fran-ti-cally burying money in his back garden.'

'Really good reading, Poppy. Now it's your turn, Darcy.' Dad beckons me with the uncooked spaghetti.

I could do with a distraction from the future horror of living off cabbage and apples for ever when I am a vegetarian, so I slump back in my seat and say, 'Fine.'

'Read this line . . .' Dad says.

Whoa! The lines are all a bit blurry, I'm thinking. *This*

16

is really far away. I squint. *This can't be right; Poppy's letters must have been so much bigger than mine. This is ridiculous. This is NOT a fair test.*

'Come on then, monkey,' Dad ushers me along.

'All right, hold your unicorns!' I yelp.

'It's actually hold your *horses*, Darcy,' Poppy says, all show-offy because she is so clever and not one bit blind. Still at least she is *thing*-less, but then again she does get to eat ham.

'Shut up, Poppy, OK . . .' I squint and move my head as close as I can to the wall so that I'm almost tipping over. 'PLANE . . . ALMOST . . . CRASHES INTO . . . EXOTIC FLAMINGO SALOON.'

'When did that happen?' Mum looks over at us, alarmed.

'It didn't!' Dad laughs. 'Come on, Darcy, take it

17

seriously. It's just a game, but at least *try*.'

'I did,' I say, going red. 'I said what I could see.'

'Darcy, it says: "Plane almost crashes into England Football Stadium".'

I look back at Dad's makeshift eye test and the words fuzz and bundle together and suddenly make sense.

Everybody looks my way.

'I'll call the optician in the morning,' Mum sighs.

NOOOOOOOOOOOOOOOOOOOOOOOOOO!

Hector and Poppy have been singing the nursery rhyme *Three Blind Mice* at me for nearly two hours. I want to punch them both in the back and wind them until approximately all their air is sucked out of them and they are empty and exhausted like deflated balloons. But really I just have to concentrate on not getting spectacles.

I can't get glasses. *Glasses?* Lots of people think they look amazing and make you look super-clever with brains that are so GINORMOUS they hardly fit into your head. But not me. I don't understand how I've shifted from awesome, amazing chick of wonderful elegance and Princess mermalade-ness to a geekazoid glasses-wearing vegetarian. I am grumpy and go to sleep with Lamb-Beth sprawled across my chest like a fluffy heavy heart, and a zillion thoughts fluttering through my head. Livid.

Chapter Two

'Hello, Darcy, my name's Anisha and I'm going to be checking your eyes today,' says the optician, leading me to a dark room. Dad is acting like a child and slurping his McDonald's milkshake extra loud – it is like a volcano in my skull.

Obviously I had to be bribed with lunch from McDonald's to get me here. I always choose nuggets because they look exactly like boots, and when you dip them in the sauce it's like getting mud on the boots. Oh. The nuggets were *chicken* nuggets. Great.

I am already a rubbish veggie and more crosserer at Dad for not reminding me that I am a vegetarian. I scowl and then I have to sit and look through these unfashionable binoculars until I see the picture on the screen of the air balloon get closerer and closerer, then tell her when it goes out of focus.

'That's great,' says Anisha, but I'm thinking, *What's great? Great that I need glasses, or great that I don't?*

Next I have to sit on this wretched plastic school chair and cover one eyeball with my hand and say the letters that I can see out loud. They are all letters in an unorganized jumble, *not* in alphabetical order and not spelling out any particular word, so it's extra hard.

P H V X B R U O N J

'That's great,' says Anisha. What's great? Did I do good or not? How do I know Anisha is not getting a serious slice of commission pie and wants me to have to buy all the glasses in the shop? So yes, it would be terrifically *great* for Anisha if I was a bit blind. 'And now try these . . .' Anisha shines a light towards the back of the screen and more letters come up.

I H A T E T H I S

'I hate this,' I say out loud.

'Darcy!' Dad coughs his milkshake up.

'What?' I gawp.

'You hate what?'

'I hate this.'

'That's not what it says.' Dad is a bit annoyed.

'Well, it's what I sawed.'

'No, "saw",' Dad says.

'Yes, I did.'

'No,' Dad growls. '*Saw*.'

'How about you stop telling me what I sawed?'

'It's saw. When you see something you say *saw*, not sawed. See, *saw*.'

I get stern. 'Dad, this isn't really the time for fun and games, we're not in the playground, my eyesight is on the line here. This is not appropriate behaviour' – *Oh, SORRY about me sounding SO growed up here like an excellent mature Queen*. Dad gulps, I point my finger at him. 'Act your age and stop slurping on that milkshake like a five-year-old. As you were, Anisha.'

'This is ridiculous,' Dad snaps, folding his arms. He is impatient now. I can hear his mind clicking away getting all itchy. 'You're wasting my time, I'm

  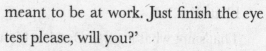

meant to be at work. Just finish the eye test please, will you?'

'Don't worry, I have what I need.' Anisha smiles sweetly. 'Why don't you go through to the waiting area and I'll process this for you.'

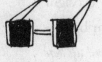

We walk out into the main waiting bit where there are hundreds of thousands of every type of glasses all lined up – people are trying them on and looking at themselves in mirrors. Like a fancy-dress shop for only secretaries and doctors.

I hate glasses, and Dad is mad, mad, mad with me. Though if I was with Mum right now I would be so even MORE in trouble, so in trouble it's not even worth thinking about actually.

 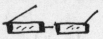

'Can't believe you did that,' Dad shout-whispers to me.

'Did what?' I say, and stare at all the other people choosing their glasses.

'You shouldn't mess around with stuff like that, it's your vision, doll, it's important. Not a joke.'

'Jokes make people laugh,' I snort. And then suddenly I see right at the back of the room, on the shelf, a rose amongst the thorns, the most incredible pair of glasses I've ever seen. Big multi-coloured, glittery rainbow, heart-shaped numbers with diamond twinkly bits around the outside that are simply so jaw-droppingly fantastic they make my heart scatter.

'I love them!' I scream. I run to try them on and pour my face into the mirror area. *Fantastic*, I'm thinking. *I look fan-tas-tic.* Dad begins to giggle.

'I think they're just for display, monkey.'

'I don't think they are.' (They are.)

'You'd wear them to school, would you?' Dad says, all sarcastic.

'Course!' I bellow across the spectacle room. 'Why wouldn't I? They are SO COOL.' Some other people look towards me just in case I happen to have found some glasses that everybody wants, but it's OK, they quickly turn back round again: only I want these babies.

'They are pretty groovy,' says Dad, and then immediately apologizes when he sees my frowning face. 'Sorry for saying the word *groovy*.'

'It's all right,' I reassure him. 'It's easy for words to jump out when you're overexcited.'

These dream glasses are so perfect for *me* that I just want to keep trying them on over and over. I can't wait to need glasses now and wear these every day and look immediately like an absolutely fabulous boss. I can't wait for Anisha to diagnose me and say those three magic words:

'*You* need glasses.'

'You *need* glasses.'

'You need *glasses*.'

Then I can walk out of here ready for whatever life throws at me. Most writers wear glasses anyway so it's only correct that I own a pair.

I get all excited thinking about all the new things I'm about to see with my all-seeing new eyes. I will zoom in like a telescope on absolutely everything and feel exactly like a wonderful spy beast. I hear Anisha's clip-cloppy shoes coming round the corner towards us so I know it's time to prepare myself – the glasses wink at me from across the room like, *See you soon, pal.*

'Darcy, it's good news,' she says. *See?* I look at Dad. I knew she wanted me to have glasses all along. 'Your eyesight is perfect and you do not need any glasses today.'

'Terrific news. Thank you,' Dad says. 'Right, come on then, monkey, home time.'

'What?' I say, aghast. 'But what about these glasses?'

'But you don't need glasses.'

'I think I do. Remember how badly I read the article on the wall yesterday?'

'Yes, but maybe you were tired.'

'I think I should retake the eye test.'

'There's no need; the lady said we didn't need to. Come on.' Dad smiles and thanks Anisha.

'But what about when I read *I HATE THIS* out loud? Remember that? Do you remember?' I try to remind Dad.

'So that WAS delib-
erate?' Dad's eyebrows
meet each other to make
one angry eyebrow (*Hi,
how are you? Yeah, not too
bad, not too bad*), and I
keep my mouth zipped
up like a grandma's
purse.

I trail away from the glasses. It's not OK now you're my age to throw yourself on the floor in crying sobs if you don't get your own way; so instead I nod and wave goodbye to the spectacles that would have changed my life.

Goodbye, life-changing spectacles. Goodbye.

*

ALL THE KIDS IN MY CLASS

All the kids in my class
They know what they're up to,
Pretending they need glasses
When they can see it all.

All the kids in my class
Pretend they can't really see,
But with a pair of glasses
They are, in fact, set free.

One kid has these spectacles
That transport him to outer space
Where he dines on planets,
On the moon, draws a smiley face.

Another has these round things
That grant her x-ray vision,
Where she can see the bones
    of all of us
And the wires inside the
    television.

This other boy has glasses
That make him hold his breath
For as long as he needs
Without ever meeting death.

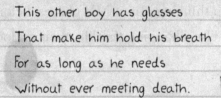

This boy uses his specs
To make him a fantastic cook,
Whilst this girl can sleep behind hers
But look like she's reading a book.

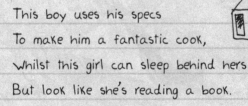

The quiet librarian, she
Tries to look soooooo busy
But her glasses are really
Taking her on safari.

All the kids in my class
They know what they're up to,
Pretending they need glasses
When they can see it all.

I can't stop thinking about MY glasses, belonging to somebody else, changing *their* life, their outlook on the world.

Chapter Three

'What is that smell?' Mum asks as she walks into the kitchen. She has on new Swedish slippers that Dad got her from Portobello Market that she will NOT take off. You can hear her feet scraping the floor with the soles of them. She is right, there is a smell in the kitchen; like Parmesan cheese or sick or horrid things all squelched together.

'Have you left something horrible in the oven?' Dad asks, because a few times Mum has left some terribly disgustingly offensive and ancient things in the oven like half-eaten plates of roast dinner (that she intends to finish nibbling on) or whole Indian takeaways.

Mum opens the oven. 'No,' she sighs, almost sad that there isn't anything old for her to eat.

'Fridge?'

'Um . . .' Mum flops over to the fridge and it opens with the globbery slobbery pulling noise it makes. 'A few jars and bits of cheese but nothing that would smell this bad.'

'Maybe Lamb-Beth had an accident?' Dad suggests.

'Er . . . or maybe she SO did NOT!' I shout. 'She never has an accident, she is a glorious clean girl, aren't you, Lamb-Beth?' Lamb-Beth at this point, perfectly timed, does a huge popping explosive fart and it stinks like rancid stew.

'And there's the answer to my question.' Dad folds the newspaper in that *I do have a point* kind of way.

'It really isn't like her to do a poo in the kitchen . . . but I suppose we should look, in case it's under one of the cabinets, rotting away.' Mum tilts her head at Dad. 'I say *we*, but I mean you.'

'What, so I'VE got to find this *missing* poo, have I?'

Mum nods and Dad rolls up his sleeves.

Not even one minute had gone by and Dad bellows, 'There we go!'

'Did you find it?' I ask.

'Not quite . . . but I sure found the culprit.'

'What is it?' Mum asks. I can hear the rumbles of Poppy and Hector now hurdling their way down the stairs, wanting to get in on the goss.

There, dangling in between Dad's fingers, is a tiny dead MOUSE.

'We've got mices!' Hector yells.

''Fraid so,' Dad says as he inspects the mouse.

'Yuck! Put it down!' Poppy screams. 'It's scary.' This encourages Dad to start pretending to throw the dead mouse at us and make terrifying noises until we are screaming our heads off.

'What do we do?' Mum asks.

'Call the police!' Hector cries.

'No, honey, you don't call the police if you have mice.'

'Oh.' Hector looks disappointed – policemen are his latest craze. I think he would faint with excitement if the police had to come over.

Dad thinks he is a bit of a policeman detective right now. He is rubbing his chin and then he says, 'Set traps, poison, that sort of thing,' and he begins wrapping the dead mouse in loads of plastic bags like what people have to do with evidence. This is too much for me to deal with on my quest to become a vegetarian. I have to swallow a ball of my own sick.

'What are you going to do with that now?' I ask, disgusted.

'Thought I might keep it as an ornament,' he

laughs with sarcasm and I scrunch my face up – there's no way that's going on our Christmas tree!

'Joking, Darcy! I'm going to throw it in the bin.' He then throws the mouse into the bin, alongside the tea bags and toast crusts.

'Just like that?' I squeal.

'Just like that,' he says, washing his hands at the sink. 'Right, who's coming to the shops with me?'

I just love supermarkets. I think they are glorious palaces with everything inside that anybody could ever want to meet in the World of Food. I like imagining everybody's shopping lists – which brand of washing powder they choose, which flavour crisps is their favourite. People always magically seem so happy in the supermarket, it is such a peaceful safe place full of beeps and human beings and *food*.

My favourite aisle is the bakery section, followed by the sweets and chocolate aisle, followed by cereal, followed by crisps. Then I like the party aisle which has everything you'd ever need to have at a party: cake mixes, candles, paper hats, those blowy things that make the surprising noise, party poppers and all different colourful plates. I love parties.

But sadly we are not in need of these aisles.

We go to the evil end, right at the back of the supermarket, next to the plain simple bottled water and cat litter, to get the mouse poison. I am a bit embarrassed; I don't want people to think we live in a disgusting unclean house that's absolutely riddled to the roof-tops with mice and infestations. We recently had a massive outcry of nits at my new school and everybody took it really seriously and got so embarrassed. At my old school we had a nit infestation rampage on a daily basis, so we were completely used to it, in fact you felt left out if you *didn't* have nits. Anyway, I remember the school nurse saying, 'Nits only like clean hair, so if you have nits that is because your hair is clean.' But I suspect this was only to try and make us feel better, and I just don't think the same rule applies to a mouse infestation.

Back home and the poison is all laid out in the cupboards and corners: it is called 'pasta bait'. It is really funny that mice enjoy pasta; I never would have thought that. Plus it's bright blue – those mice are *so* fussy. They will be wanting candlelit dinners next and bread baskets!

'I thought mice liked cheese?' Poppy asks while we are unpacking the shopping. So did I actually, but I'll leave her to find out the answer and look stupid.

'I think they like most things,' Dad says. 'Look at this!' He is holding up Mum's hand cream that lives by the kitchen sink – all around the side of the tube are tiny teeth-sized munch marks. 'See those nibbles on the side – they've even tried to get in there!'

Hand Cream

'It's because it's coconut flavour,' I suggest.

'Funny how mice like cheese and when they die they smell like cheese. I think that means I'll smell like apple juice and chocolate cake when I die,' Poppy ponders. 'Trust us to get the ones that like blue pasta and moisturizer.'

In bed I keep thinking I can hear the scurrying tiptoeing of a mouse in my room. I just CANNOT be bothered to find a mouse crawling over my face whilst I sleep and using my open snoring mouth as some kind of basin to wash its paws in. EUGH!

Maybe the mouse might even
attempt using my tongue
as a slide when I sleep?
Like some kind of
outrageously fantastic
water slide? What if
they start taking turns
and one accidentally falls
down my throat and it gets trapped and then it has to
live in my tummy and that becomes its new flat and
I have to go about the rest of my life with a mouse
living in my belly? Imagine how much it will hurt
when it wants to decorate? Or put pictures up? I'm
going to have to be a really strict killjoy landlord.

A screeching 'AHHHHHHHHH!'
wakes us all up an hour earlier than
normal. It's Poppy.

We all know that 'AHHHHHHHHHH!' very well, because it's the same one she does when she goes on her bike or it's her birthday or she has a bee near her or sees a pop star she likes on the TV.

This time, she's seen a mouse.

'I was just eating some cereal and then I saw it scamper across the kitchen floor. It was so fast. It made me jump!' Suddenly Mum and I begin curling our toes up, it's almost like our feet and legs begin to get itchy and irritated. It's as if we can feel hundreds of tiny mouse hands and feet all over our skin. Now I know why that lady in the *Tom and Jerry* cartoons gets so angry and is always marching around with that broomstick.

'Which way did it go?' asks Dad.

'That way,' says Poppy, pointing to the cellar.

We all head down to the horrid cave dungeon, Mum carrying Hector. It smells damp and it's all dark and cobwebby. It is also home to lots of boring shed tools, boxes of beer, raincoats and wellington boots, but I am very good at seeing the potential in

things and realize it could be an excellent den.

'I'M SCARED!' Poppy squeals and runs back up.

'It's cool down here!' I say brightly.

'Yeah, freezing.' Mum wraps her cardigan around her and Hector.

'I meant cool as in . . . good. I like it.'

But she is already heading back upstairs, asking who wants a cup of tea. I don't know why she even offers us tea because tea actually means: a coffee for Dad, orange squash for Poppy and Hector, water for me and a cup of tea just for herself. Really it should be, 'Who wants a squash?' because that's the most popular choice. You wouldn't say, 'Who wants a slice of pizza?' when you know nobody else eats pizza. Although that's a terrible example because who doesn't eat pizza?

I stick with Dad in the cool cellar, plotting my idea for a hideaway or den. A lick of paint, some cushions, a little writing desk, perhaps a lava lamp and a beanbag and we will be well and truly golden . . . well, after the mouse infestation has passed.

'How do the mice get up into the kitchen if they live down here? It's not as if the door is open,' I ask.

'Mice can get into gaps the size of pinheads, their backs are bendy like shoelaces and they can wriggle into the tiniest of holes, the nippers.' I can tell Dad's a bit enjoying this new hobby; he gets a whole pot of the bright blue pasta bait and plonks it in the centre of the cellar. 'That will do the trick. Not all mice eat on the spot, they sometimes take the bait back to their nests, to feed their family.'

'Awww, that's thoughtful of them,' I say.

'Hmm . . . not in this case, Darcy.'

'Yeah, it's like a takeaway.'

'Yeah, but would you think it was nice of me if I came back from the Chinese takeaway with poisonous noodles? I don't think so!'

'Poison!' I cry. I love animals, remember.

'What? Did you think I was feeding them? Fattening them up for a competition? Come on, Darcy, they aren't our pets!'

'But Dad, it seems so unfair and so not like what a nice human being would do.'

'OK . . . look . . .' Dad sighs. 'Here's what we shall do. I don't want to hurt the animals, I just don't know how else to get them out of our home . . . so, I'll buy you a little cage and you can try and collect the mice yourself. Every mouse you catch you can put in the cage and you can keep it as a pet. How does that sound?'

'OK. Fine,' I say.

'Yeah?'

'Yeah.'

Dad strokes my hair. 'Come on then, monkey, let's have some breakfast . . . if the mice haven't got there first, that is!' He makes his way up the stairs. 'Oh, and by the way, you're not a nice human *being*, you are a nice human *bean* . . . because you're a vegetarian. Ha-ha-ha.'

Oh ha-ha-ha-ha-ha-ha-ha. So funny I forgot to laugh.

Chapter Four

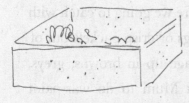 As promised, Dad makes a little cage out of a cardboard box. It has straw all along the bottom, cotton-wool-type fluff and even a water dispenser.

'What's that?' Poppy demands the moment her eyes clap on it. 'It better NOT be for a hamster. I've been asking for a hamster for SO long, and already Darcy hogs Lamb-Beth to death, so this better not be more pets for her.'

'Calm down,' says Dad. 'It's for all three of you. Darcy doesn't like the idea of the mice getting poisoned, so I've said you guys can keep whatever mice you manage to catch in here as pets.'

You can almost hear Lamb-Beth gulp – she is clearly concerned.

We make Dad get our fishing nets out of the boot of the car. It's a weird place for nets to live but they just seem to have made a home for themselves there (because, let's face it, what are we going to catch with nets in London? Carrier bags or crisp packets out of the puddles?). We camouflage up in browns, greys, greens and blacks and ask Mum to do war-paint camouflage lines on our faces like true safari hunters. We are ready for action. For the rest of the day we lurk, hunt, snoop, spy and sneak as much as we can.

'You do know that mice are nocturnal, don't you, my babies?' Mum calls out as we slip down the stair-case like jungle shadows.

'SHHHHHH!' I growl, not wanting the mice to know we are literally on their tail. 'We are on *call*.'

'Sor-ry,' Mum whispers back.

I hate asking for help when I want to be in charge but I ask Mum, 'What does nocturnal mean?'

'It means they only come out at night.'

I huff. Great. 'So I'll be sleeping whilst they are out, probably, won't I?'

'Probably, yes,' Mum says. 'That's why they are so tricky to be rid of. That's why I'm packing everything into the lunch boxes, so they can't get in.' Mum has turned the kitchen upside down and all the cereal, rice and (normal-coloured, so jealous of those mice) pasta is in boxes and tubs.

'We're never going to catch ANY mice at this rate. Will you maybe let us stay up one tiny bit later, just until it gets really dark, to see if we can catch at least one?'

'If you're good and you come and help me with this,' she replies.

So all three of us get demoted from catching mice to packing the food into boxes, but it's OK because Mum has the radio on really loud and we all do singing and stuff and then we eat a bowl of cereal as a reward.

Night time takes for ever to come but the kitchen is spotless and smells like bleach. We are not even allowed one snack without completely tidying every crumb around us. Personally it seems a little late to begin telling us off for crumbs, as we've already got mice, but Mum says she thinks it will only help make them leave sooner if they can't find food. Lamb-Beth's bowl of greens has moved to outside the kitchen door, but I don't think she minds. She hasn't said anything to me about it anyway.

We can't really be bothered to dress back up into our camouflage and so we continue to snoop in our pyjamas. Hector really isn't used to being up late so he is really hyper and over the top and squealing and being the worst mouse-catcher ever.

'They can feel your vibrations, you know!' I snap at him. But he doesn't care. I just keep looking at the mice cage that should be full to the brim of pet mice all having a luxurious time, but it is as empty as our biscuit tin. If only the mice knew that we were only trying to help them, then perhaps they would understand and give themselves up. But then again they might not trust us and anyway, most importantly, I can't speak mouse language. Fuming.

'I KNOW!' says Poppy. 'Let's tell Lamb-Beth what we want to say to the mice and she can pass the message on to them that we come in peace and we only want to protect them and love them.'

'How will Lamb-Beth know what to say?'

'She's an animal, duh. Have you ever seen that film *Babe*, about the pig?'

'No . . .' I am well jels now.

'I watched it at Timothy's, but basically, all animals can speak animal language and it's about this pig . . . but I can't remember its name.'

'Er, let me guess,' I say with sarcasm. 'Babe?'

'Oh, yeah. The pig is called Babe.' She smiles all goofy and I roll my eyes in impatience. 'So you just need to tell Lamb-Beth what the message is and she can pass it on to the mouses . . . I mean, mice.'

'Good idea, but how will Lamb-Beth know what we are saying to *her*?'

'She's fluent in both human and animal for goodness' sake, as she's lived with us long enough. It's like when Uncle Adrian moved to New York and learned how to speak American so quickly, remember?'

'Poppy, American is the same as English.'

'Oh, I just thought he was really clever. Oh well, OK, but it's worth a try anyway.'

Lamb-Beth is snoring away on Mum's lap. We gently wake her up and peel her off.

'Oi, she was keeping me warm,' Mum moans.

'We need her for a real quick sec,' I say.

'Don't disturb her, you lot.'

We ignore Mum and get back to work. We prop Lamb-Beth up by the cage, so she can get a good old look at it and hopefully recommend it as suitable accommodation to the mice.

'Hi, LAMB-BETH,' I start, really loudly and slowly and clearly.

'Don't speak to her like she's an idiot!' Poppy nudges me. 'Move over. You are patronizing her.'

GGGGGGRRRRR, Poppy and her stupid clever words. *Who does she even think she is?*

All of a sudden Poppy transforms into what I can only describe as a full-blown geezer, exactly like the builders at the house at the end of our road.

'Hey, Lamb-Beth, right, not wanting to cause too much of a fuss or upheaval here, sure you've heard the gossip and it's all true. Yes, I can reveal, we have, you've guessed it, got mice. Riddled. I mean top to bottom, place full of 'em. So myself and my siblings here, who you know very well, would like to ask a favour of you, seeing as we do favours for you like cleaning up your poo and stuff, if you wouldn't mind simply passing a message on to the mice, if you see them?'

Lamb-Beth stares blankly at Poppy and then slow blinks.

'Perfect, thanks, mate,' Poppy continues.

'She didn't say yes.'

'Yes, she did!'

'When?'

'She blinked!'

'KIDS!' Dad shouts. 'Enough, enough. Bed.'

'But, Dad!' I yell back. 'We're so close to catching a mouse.'

'I'm sorry, come on, no fighting, it's past your bedtime, come on now. Brush your teeth, up we go, let's go.'

'Pllllleeeeeeeeeeaaaaaaaaasssssssssseeeeeeee . . . just five more minutes?' Poppy pleads.

'Nope. Don't push it, come on, upstairs.'

I am well fed up. Not as in full up from food over-load – as in disappointed. I am in a right grump.

Ring, ring, ring, goes my rubbish alarm, which means it's Monday morning and time for school. Being big means that I'm at bigger school with loads of important stuff to do and know about. I'm basically Darcyopedia these days. I think people make up facts all the time anyway; there is no possible way on those nature programmes that the scientist actually truly knows what is going on inside a maggot's brain – I mean, it's not like they can *interview* the maggot. Or when they say, 'Here is the tiger, gently approaching the antelope, preparing to capture its prey.' How do they know the tiger and antelope aren't just really good friends actually, and all the tiger wants to do is get a piggyback off the antelope?

When I get downstairs Dad is making coffee with a very cheeky grin on his face.

'Morning, Dad.'

'Morning, Darcy.'

'You look happy.'

'I am.'

Mum does a sideways smile-meets-eyebrow face, like the faces they do on quiz shows when they already know what the answer is but they are being polite and letting the quiz master finish the question before answering it correctly.

57

'He's very excited, aren't you?' Mum says.

'Wouldn't say excited . . . just interested.' Dad pours the hot smoky brown coffee (blended-up monster poo) into his and Mum's cups. I can't wait to start needing coffee and having a set of door keys because it means you've truly *made* it.

'Why?' I pour my cereal into the bowl. Poppy and Hector are already crunching away.

'Because he is looking forwarded to peeking his eyes inside the poison pot to seed if he killed any of the mices,' Hector says whilst watching the morning cartoons – we've had to get a mini-TV put in the kitchen for Hector or otherwise he doesn't eat his breakfast.

'Oh, really?' I am furious.

'Yes, he is going to look after we've gonned for school as well.'

'THAT IS NOT FAIR!' I bark.

'Er. Did somebody get out of the wrong side of bed?' Mum squeaks.

'No, I got out the side of bed I always get out of because there is a wall against the other side. So technically what you have suggested is NOT POSSIBLE.'

'What's the matter then?'

'Him!' I point at Dad.

'Me?'

'Yes.'

'What did I do?' Dad slurps his coffee, knowing exactly full *well* what he did.

'A mixture of absolutely wretched things.'

'Like what?'

'Firstly, killing the mice and being excited about it.'

'I didn't say I was excited, Darcy. Mum said that. *I* said I was *interested.*'

'Fine. Well, you're interested in killing mice and that's really bad.'

'We've been through this, remember? Otherwise

they can run wild in the house. What would you rather? That they nibble up all your writing books and Mum's moisturizer and eat out of Lamb-Beth's food bowl?'

'Course not! You just don't have to be all haps about the whole thing.'

'I'm not HAPS. In an ideal world we don't have mice in our house, they live in the fields and forests and we live here. What else is in the *cocktail of wretched things of why you are annoyed*?'

'That YOU get to catch them whenever you want but you didn't even let us try and catch until a bit later on last night, and therefore our cage is empty.'

'That actually annoyed me too,' Poppy pipes up. 'That was out of order.'

'You had school this morning, you had long enough to catch the mice. Back me up please, Mollie.'

'I'm not getting involved,' Mum says, and finishes packing Poppy's lunch in tinfoil.

'AND you never told us that mices were day-allergic even though you knew that.'

Dad laughs. 'It seems the only person here who is day-allergic is you! You need to go back to bed and try restarting the day over.'

'I'm not finished. And THEN, on top of all of that, you thought you would look to see if the mice had taken the poison when we were all at school, so we would miss out.'

'I just know the morning time is a rush.'

'Still. It's selfish.'

'OK, I'll wait till later on, and we can all look before dinner.'

'You won't wait,' Poppy argues. 'You can't even wait for your toast to get toasted properly and that's why your toast is always rawed and soggy.'

'They do have a point . . .' Mum giggles.

'OK, so let's look now.'

'Well . . . fine.'

I was quite surprised at this. We never get to do anything other than get ready for school in get-ready-for-school hour.

We all creep down and it's as if that scary music from the shark film *Jaws* is behind us and we are little action figurines tiptoeing over the top, down into the cellar, one after the other. The tension rises as the stuffy smell of the damp basement hits us like a wall. It's like walking into a dust cloud.

'I don't like it.' Poppy runs back up again, but not me or Hector, we're *brave*. Dad shines his torch now and it beams all over the room in golden pyramids. I start to feel all itchy again, as though the mice are running up my legs and in my hair. My heart begins to beat a bit louder. I feel like giggling even though nothing is funny, but my tummy is doing cartwheels and swishing about like I've eaten loads of popcorn kernels and they are exploding in my stomach. Dad crouches down next to the big tub of blue pasta bait and then he lifts the lid off.

And inside, the pasta has been completely eaten so there are just a few crumbs and there are six or seven mice all *hanging out* inside the pot.

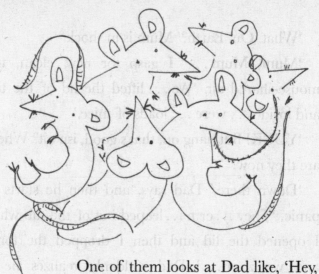

One of them looks at Dad like, 'Hey, man, shut the lid, dude.' *AHHHHHH!* Dad drops the lid and we all run out and upstairs as quick as can be, and we are screaming and screaming.

'What. On. Earth?' Mum is in shock.

'Mum, Mum . . .' I gasp for new, clean, not mouse-shared air. 'We . . . lifted the lid of the tub and inside . . . were . . . loads of mice.'

'YUCK! But hang on, that's good, isn't it? Where are they now?'

'Down there,' Dad says, and then he starts to panic. 'They . . . erm . . . leaped out of the tub when I opened the lid and then I dropped the torch and we . . . er . . .' Dad suddenly realizes he is sounding quite feeble and weak. 'Then I, er . . . thought the kids should be getting off to school and so I . . .' I look at Dad in disbelief; he really is a cheeky biscuit.

'Hmmm. I heard you scream the loudest.' Mum nudges Dad; she loves to show him up.

'Oh, really?' he answers in a squeaky high-pitched tingly shrill. 'I mean, oh really?' He makes his voice go all extra-deep, gravelly and cavemanlike, just like the voices that do the voiceovers on trailers in the cinema. 'I was just supporting the kids. Of course.'

I feel sad. Imagine if WE were mices and some-body dreaded and wretched was trying their best to kill us! If only I could catch one, rescue it and keep it as my pet.

On the way to school, I pull out my notebook and start writing . . .

Mummy Mouse was a really good mouse and even better at being a mum. She took excellent care of her husband and the three children they had together: Nancy, Lily and Oscar. On Fridays she cooked the most delicious vegetarian pie, stuffed to the top with sweet potato, pumpkin and parsnip, topped with strong, powerful cheese. She would cover the top with freshly-made pastry, fork the edges to seal the roof and then she would glaze the

top with a milky swash of egg-wash to give it
a glossy shine. It would wait on the counter
until tea time and then it would meet the
roaring heat of the blistering oven (a hairdryer)
and become the most scrumptious pie in
the world.

'Tea time!' Mummy Mouse squeaked. 'The
pie is going in the oven!' and that meant that
Nancy, Lily, Oscar and their dad would
squeak even louder in hungry belly shrieks – the
pie had an important date with their tummies.
But suddenly Mummy Mouse screamed,
'AHHHHHHHHH!'

'What's the matter?' asked her husband.

'L-l-l-l-ook . . .'

'Where?'

'Th-th-th-th-there, on the pie top.'

And so her husband went over to see the
pie, the oven blazing behind
him, and that was when
he saw the fingerprints.

The unmistakable fingerprints of one thing and one thing only. A human being.

'Oh dear!' Daddy Mouse screeched.

'I know, isn't it disgusting? The pie is ruined and the house is infested!'

Nancy, Lily and Oscar bundled into the kitchen in their little twee mouse house, curious as to why their mother had screamed.

'What's happened?' Nancy asked.

'We've got *humans!*' Dad sighed.

'Don't scare the children!'

'You frightened them enough with your scream!' Dad pointed out, eyebrow rising.

Nancy suddenly felt all squirmy. Humans? *Humans.* That *was* disgusting. They were so

big and slimy and smelly. They had weird
fingers and weird toes and noses and bones.
They were bulky. They had strange boomy
voices and clumpy dompy feet. They were
strangers. Aliens. Weirdos. Horrible things.
Horrible things that wore . . . shoes.

'We have to get rid of them!' Lily yelped.

'Can't we keep one?' Nancy said. She quite
liked the idea of having a disgusting oversized
ginormous human being in her house. She could
put it in a big clear Perspex box with a water
fountain and a massive bowl of cereal for a
snack. It would be happy there. She had seen
humans at the farm and in the zoo but she
had never ever seen a real-life one. If only
she could keep one. *But how would she
catch it?*

'KEEP ONE?' Mum squealed. 'They are
vile. Have you lost your mind? Human beings
are lazy, moany, wretched creatures that
pick their noses and fart and burp. Haven't

you seen them? Itching their heads on the
sofa? Scratching their bums whilst making a
cup of tea? Sneezing? Snoring? Coughing and
spluttering. They are the worst creatures in
the world! Keep them? We should kill them
more like!'

'But Mum, that's cruel,' Nancy argued.

'This is cruel, Nancy. Look at our pie.
Dinner is ruined!'

It didn't seem fair to Nancy. If the world
had been different who's to say that Nancy
herself couldn't have been maybe borned
a human? Oscar and Lily too! It wasn't
the human's fault. She was sure it didn't
deliberately leave its fingerprints on top of
the pie . . .

But it was too
late. Nancy's dad
was already laying
the poison traps. He
knew that humans

adored sandwiches, and so Mummy Mouse
made the sandwiches and Dad laced the
fillings with a deadly poison. Next they hid the
sandwiches all over their mouse house. Their
hope would be that the humans would find
the sandwiches, eat them and then . . . croak
it! Leaving the family of mice with a beautiful
human-free house.

Nancy went to bed in her fluffy corner
of wool but she couldn't sleep. She couldn't
stand the idea of the humans finding a tasty
sandwich and eating it, getting poisoned and
then being deaded. Or worse, what if they
took the sandwiches back and gave them to
their babies? Imagine if somebody laid traps
for them, and her dad accidentally picked them
up and brought them home and she and Lily
and Oscar ate them! The thought made her
upset. She curled the little sock she slept in up
around her head to try and comfort herself
and feel cosy, but she was tossing and turning

and couldn't get comfortable. The idea of the humans eating the poison was eating her up with guilt. She had to do something.

Nancy decided that the only thing she could do to completely and safely ensure that the humans didn't eat the poison was to collect the sandwiches up herself whilst her family were sleeping.

Tiptoeing out of her sock later that night, she softly opened the drawer by the side of her bed and from it took a little crystal bead. When it caught the moonlight it made for a perfect torch. She would use the sock she slept in as a sack to collect the sandwiches up. Nancy then slipped out of her bedroom and began hunting for the sandwiches.

The sarnies did look tempting. How terrifically cruel her mum was to make them look so appealing. This infuriated her even more on the humans' behalf and she scurried even quicker, racing to pack them all up.

Nancy crept round the perimeter of the wall towards the last sandwich lurking by the skirting board, her tail swishing behind her. But suddenly she heard a voice. A *human* voice and footsteps too! A shadow began to loom over her, a shadow bigger than any you could possibly imagine. Then she saw a huge human hand with five fingers and nails and a wristwatch that told the time. Nancy's eyes bulged out of her head. This was the most scared and excited she had ever been. Even the breeze as the hand brushed past her was strong enough to steal her breath away; it was like a whale jumping over her head. She stayed perfectly exactly still and watched as the human moved. How she would *love* one for herself, to pet and feed. She would be such a good owner.

The poisoned sandwich! She must stop her pet human from eating it! She sprinted towards the sandwich and clung to it tightly. Her eyes scrunched up, her claws wrapped around it, but then up, up, up she went as the human lifted her.

AHHHHHHHHHHHHH!

The view! She had never been so high up! Nancy was terrified – her ears were muffled with all the new noises, the speed made her face nearly rip off. And before she knew it, she was eye to eye with a REAL human.

The next few moments were quite peculiar for Nancy as MORE humans came into sight. She had only ever *heard* of humans, and now there were LOADS. Mother was right, they did have an infestation. Nancy's senses were going loopy as she was met with a chaos of screaming and yelling, stomping and arguing.

This couldn't be over *her*? She was tiny compared to them – an acorn to their oak.

'Excuse me!' Nancy squeaked. 'If I could just have a moment of your time?' But her voice was drowned out by screams and yelps. 'I don't mean any harm but if you' – her squeals were not heard, she was getting impatient – 'I was hoping you might like to be my pet? Excuse me? Did you hear? Are you even listening? Have you no manners?'

The humans didn't hear. She put her hands on her hips and dropped her crystal bead. It was a long way down and it hit the floor with a crashing splintering thud.

'Look what you made me do!' she yelped at the humans. 'That will be broken now. I get the point, you do not wish to be my pet, fine, so if you wouldn't mind putting me down so that I may go home.'

In her brain she was thinking she should have just let them poison themselves on the stupid sandwiches for how unpleasant the humans were being to her, but she wasn't a nasty mouse. She certainly didn't want one for her pet any more.

'Put me DOWN!' She struggled to escape the grip of one of the humans. 'Let me go!' She wrestled and fought, anything to release herself from the grasp, but you can imagine it was useless against the human's strength and before she knew it she found herself inside a cold dark shoebox.

There wasn't much air and she was frightened. Mum and Dad would be so worried. Lily and Oscar would be so scared. She was trapped. Nancy squealed and wailed and tried with all her might to lift the lid. But it was no good. She tried to munch through the sides but the cardboard was too tough. WHY was she in the box? WHAT was going to happen next? She missed her family. Why did she have to be so stupid and curious?

Exhausted and upset, she slumped to the side of the box and eventually fell asleep.

'Hello, Yoghurt. Yoghurt! Wakey, wakey. Rise and shine!' She heard a voice. Yoghurt? What was this new word yoghurt? Nancy woke up, dazed and dreamy as the light kissed her brightly in the face when the box top was lifted. A big finger prodded her in the belly. NO. NO. NO. NO. She wriggled free of the human's touch but it just came after her and scooped her up.

'My name is NANCY!' the little mouse whimpered. 'You have me mistaken, I don't know who Yoghurt is. Who is this Yoghurt you speak of? If I could just talk to my mum and dad. Please. They are just down there, please, I think there has been a miscommunication.'

'That's a funny happy squeak you've got!' the human said, and stroked Nancy again. 'I've named you Yoghurt because your fur is soft and white and your tail is pink — you look like a little spoonful of strawberry yoghurt.' The human giggled. 'I've been busy this morning — this is your lovely new home, look, Yoghurt. I've rescued you and now you are safe. Do you like it?'

Nancy was dropped into a cage. A cage with sawdust and fluff and a bowl of dried ugly pellets. She was a pet. A prisoner herself. Nancy shook her head in total disbelief. She clung onto the cage bars, gripping tight, panicking, looking for a hole, an escape, a chink to squeeze through. *PLEASE, NO! MY*

FAMILY! PLEASE! THERE HAS BEEN A MISTAKE! I AM NOT YOGHURT. I AM NOT A PET! I AM NANCY! PLEASE, PLEASE, LET ME GO! LET ME GO!

Nancy cried and cried and ran to the fluff so that she could hide. Perhaps she would fall asleep, wake up and find out this was all some terrible, miserable dream. It had to be. This couldn't be her destiny.

'Aaah, look, you love it in there already, yes, that's your bed,' the human cooed. 'Mum! Mum, Yoghurt's already using her bed!' The human giggled again. 'And just to think, my parents were trying to poison you! But I saved you and I am going to love you for ever.'

I am actually glad that the cage at home is empty of mices. I wouldn't want to be separated from my family and live in a new home.

Chapter Five

I meet my bestest friend Will by the gates. He is peeling a tangerine.

'Hi so much!' I smile so hard I make my eyes blind with cheek chub.

'ORRRRRRGGGGH.'

Will throws his peel down.

'What did I do?'

'Jogged me.'

'Jogged you? I'm nowhere near you.'

'Jogged me with your words. I was trying to peel

this off in one go, you know, to make a spiral. Annie can do it and I can't, and just to be annoying she's leaving them all around the house to show off. It's getting on my nerves.'

'Sorry. I didn't realize.'

'It's not your fault, it's just frustrating. I've been trying all weekend.'

'Have you got any more? Let me try.'

Will hands me a tangerine and then begins chewing on his own and the juicy sunshine smell explodes into the air. 'Honestly,' he begins again, 'I've had so much vitamin C from all these tangerines and satsumas over the weekend, I'm surprised I've not turned into an orange.'

'You've got the hair for it,' I say, naturally imagining what Will would look like as an orange. It's easier than you think. We walk, as I am beginning to peel the stiff fruit, popping my thumb into the head and working my way round.

'How was your weekend?'

'Funny but annoying,' I say as we step into school.

'I feel like I never have a relaxing weekend, there is always something wild and crazy and annoying going on with my family.'

'You wouldn't want it any other way though. Believe me, if Annie goes out, sometimes I just sit in playing PlayStation and eating whole packets of cookies for hours on end. It can be well boring.'

'Sounds like a dream,' I say, but that's also because if Annie was my big sister I would probably also be sneakily going in her room, trying on her clothes and hoop earrings and perfumes.

'Oh no.' Will suddenly stops completely in his tracks, as if his feet have been cemented to the floor. He goes a translucent tracing-paper white, though his cheeks redden and his eyes water. His whole body stiffens, as if a cold current of ice has just shot through his veins, and his eyebrows get higher and higher as his chin slowly drops. He lets his school bag fall with a stinging thud and does something he rarely if ever does: grabs my arm for support or comfort or just to stop himself from actually physically falling over.

'Will, Will? What is it?' It's almost like he's a statue. I try and look ahead to see what's bothering him, but it's too busy with all the noise and commotion at the start of school on a Monday morning. Birds caw overhead followed by an aeroplane, and when the plane soars over and leaves the quiet noise behind, the school bell screams its head off, meaning it's time for registration. Through all this Will is ear-puncturing me with his silence. I shake him again. 'Will? You're scaring me, what is it?' The other kids start piling their way through the school doors and that's when I see a man, looking sad mixed with happy, waving, trying to say hello.

'It's my dad.'

Surrounded by the shrieking hum of the bell, Will allows himself to be carried towards where his dad is standing, as if hypnotized. The man's face lifts when he sees Will walk towards him and he begins to smile properly now. I take this as my cue to pick Will's bag up and rubberneck (unwanted looking or spying) as I let my jelly legs jiggle me into the building. *Should I tell Reception about Will's dad? Should I phone Annie? Should I run back out and stand next to Will? Would he even want me there?*

I decide to go up to the front desk.

'How's your lamb?' The receptionist, Mavis, is Scottish and her voice sounds like a xylophone, all plinky plonky and musical.

'She's fine. Erm . . .' I shake my head to try and focus, but I can't really get my head ironed out and my words tumble out in a jumble that went like this but at 500 miles per second:

'Will's here but he's not in here with me, he— you see, Will's here but his dad, who I think we hate but

I'm not sure because we never speak about it, who I've never met and I have known Will for years, has just turned up at the gates, the school gates, and I wanted you to know . . . what I mean is that Will has turned up for school but obviously wasn't expecting to see his dad at the other side of the gates and I was going to go over too but then I— I've got his school bag as proof, look, and his tangerine.'

'Slow down, hen . . . start again.' Mavis smiles, shifting her glasses down her nose so she can see me properly.

'Sorry.'

'Take a wee breath.' I have to remind myself that in Scottish wee means 'little'

and not 'wee wee' and that she wasn't just suggesting that my breath smelled unspeakable.

'William Hopper's dad, who he doesn't really know, has just turned up outside.'

'Was Will expecting him?'

'No, I don't think so.' I breathe out like a deflated balloon.

'OK, thanks, petal. Do you want to leave Will's bag here with me, come in and have a wee drink of something, a sweet tea or some squash maybe, and a biscuit? I've got shortbread from home. I'll call Security.'

'Security?'

'Yes, love. Will's dad can't just turn up un-announced, it's trespassing.'

I sit down. I feel like I take up too much space in the office, with all the other staff members typing and nattering away. I feel like an intruder, an alien on another planet, like I've been let backstage at the theatre or am looking inside the engine of a car – this is the stuff you're not meant to see. I watch as Mavis punches the number for Security into the phone. The clock is ticking behind my head. My class will be wondering where I am. I'll have an absent mark put next to my name in the register. *What if they call home and tell Mum I bunked off school? Poor Will! What if his dad is upsetting him?* He might not have wanted school to know his dad turned up. *I might have ruined everything for him!*

A lady who I don't recognize comes past and places a plastic cup of orange squash in front of me, and then Mavis, who is on the phone, snaps her fingers at her. 'Tea!' she says, covering the mouthpiece. 'Nice hot sweet tea, to dunk biscuits into please . . . the shortbread, it's in my top drawer . . . would you mind fetching it? I'll have a cup too, thanks.'

The lady smiles at me sarcastically and tuts, and then walks off to make tea for our *unannounced* mini tea party.

Mavis winks at me. 'Can't have shortbread without tea,' she whispers, then considers. 'Can't have tea without short-bread . . . ah, yes!' She goes back into conversation on the phone and I am left with sweaty palms and watering eyes wondering

what is happening outside with Will and his dad.

I feel guilt swallow me up. We never talk about Will's parents. I have only ever seen one photograph of Will and Annie's mum, and that lives by the TV in their living room. I have been to Will's house fewer times than the  amount of fingers I have because Will gets a bit weird about people being there. In the picture Annie and Will are smallerer, Will is just a toddler and Annie is about eight. She still looks exactly the same and Will looks even more ginger. They are both wearing their pyjamas and it looks like it's Christmas Day because everybody seems happy and there is crumpled-up wrapping paper on the floor. Will's mum has an arm around them both, like a bird with a chick in each wing. Her face is a picture of a new kind of happiness. Walt Disney couldn't even create this kind of wild smile. The eyes are twinkling and shining and her hair is bright red and curly and framing her face like a border of red roses. She is probably the most real-life prettiest person I have ever known other than my own mum.

I think Will and Annie's mum died the year after that photograph was taken because Will says he doesn't really even remember her. But Annie does, I am sure. Will said he thinks she was ill even in that picture but it's difficult to imagine because she looks so joyful. I didn't know anything about Will's dad other than he lived in the countryside with a new girl-friend and some new babies. I don't think Annie and Will like their dad very much because whenever they mention him (which is rarer than seeing a shooting star) the other one rolls their eyes in annoyance or changes the subject. There are not any photographs of their dad anywhere in the house, but I bet he was the photographer of the picture by the TV. The one where everybody is smiling back into the lens, happy to be together.

My thoughts are broken when I am ushered back to class with the taste of milky tea in my throat and the sugar granules of shortbread frosted around my mouth. My class teacher, Mrs Ixy, isn't one bit cross with me, and she takes me to our English class personally so she can walk in with me and check everything is OK. I hope Will is OK.

English was the subject we all thought I'd be best at because of my writing, but if you didn't know already there is this whole entire other half to English which is all about tenses and nouns and verbs and punctuation and grammar and spelling and it actually isn't just, 'Hey, let's read from this great book all morning.' And so now it's become a bit harder for me. Because I can't spell very good, or do grammar either.

I panic in the classes where I used to be as cool as a carrot. Or is it a cucumber? I just can't remember and I don't even know what makes cucumbers so much cooler than the rest of us. Maybe it's because they come with a drink inside their bodies . . . they should make crisps with drinks inside the bags, don't you think? So when you get thirsty from all the salty munching it's already there and waiting to be drunk? I'm so exhausted by my genius brain and instead of 'finding the grammatical errors' in the paragraph that Mr Yates has given us, I imagine that I will become really high up at the Palace of Ideas and then I can leave this boring school at the drop of a scarf … or is it a hat? Whatever. I find the tangerine from earlier in my pocket and start peeling it again. The peel is coming away from the flesh in a lovely winding curl, like ribbon or a pig's tail that just keeps turning and turning. I'm trying so major hard not to tear the peel so that it comes off in one fancy impressive spiral. One that will really impress Will when he's back. Peeling is about patience and confidence … I guess that's what life is about too.

Peel. Peel. Peel. My head trails off into a dreamy place …

The streets are oily and dark, wet from rain. The pavement is glossy, the brickwork on buildings is crumbling and derelict, but they look drawn-on, like in pencil or charcoal. Smoke blooms out of the busted, broken-down engine of a car that has smashed into a lamp-post, which has crumpled to the floor. The light hasn't gone off, it still shines, painting amber honey squares across the midnight street, good enough to eat. Mice, millions of them, swarm out of the gutter, the drains, from underneath the cracks in doors. They move like a rippling wave, their combined squeaks sounding more like screeching foxes. I watch from the top of a tall building, the rain in my hair, trying to figure out in the blinding darkness where they are going, until I see a sign with an arrow. It says WILL – THIS WAY, and the mice run towards it . . .

'Darcy! Darcy? Hello, anybody home? DARCY BURDOCK?'

'Huh?' I wobble out of my chair.

'I said, how many grammatical errors did you spot in the paragraph?' Mr Yates shoves his big round face close to mine, his hands all clasped together in an *I know the answer to everything* kind of way.

'Erm. Lots?'

The class erupts into deep brain-frying laughter.

'How many is *lots* then, Darcy?'

'Like *loads*?' I panic. Everybody is staring at me, and the paragraph in front of me is untouched, with fewer marks on it than a brand-new pair of trainers.

'So when somebody asks you . . . say, for example . . . how old you are . . . would you say *lots* or *loads*?' The laughter comes again, like a water pistol of embarrassment shooting me straight in the face.

'No.' I am defensive, my back straightens up.

'So why would you use it now? I want you to be specific.' He's getting right on my nerves. I'm about to pop, I'll risk it now, get into trouble for it, I don't care, all I care about is Will right now.

'OK, I'll be specific, I found none. I found NO grammatical errors in the paragraph!' I shout, and then add in my head, BECAUSE I WASN'T PAYING ATTENTION.

And the class goes quiet.

'Correct answer.' Mr Yates slaps his thigh in teacherish pleasure. I am in shock. 'The truth is, this paragraph is grammatically correct. It was a trick test!'

The class protests in chorus, complaining and

95

moaning and tutting and sighing and throwing me jealous evils.

'Looks like somebody has been working really hard this year, great work, Darcy.' Mr Yates collects up the paragraphs, mine being the only one untouched. I look down at my tangerine peel, only to see I have removed the whole peel from the fruit in one. *Yesssssssssssss!*

It's lunch time and Will still hasn't come back into class and Mavis can't give me any more information, though she does say, 'If I hear anything at all you'll be the first to know.'

I sellotape the tangerine peel into my writing book, as I am worried it might get damaged if I leave it to roll around my bag unsupervised. Then I decide to trace the outline of the peel in black marker: should it go missing I will then have some visual evidence that I did create it. Then I hear lots of hushed laughter and snickering happening in a huddle near to me and I look up and see wretched Clementine, the WORST girl from America, telling a story. A big gaggle of girls are all listening to her every word as she pulls some faces that could easily be in the most annoying faces in the 'hall of fame of annoying faces' that I have ever seen. I try to make out what they are talking about but I just can't and I don't want to earwig in too hard in case

it seems like I CARE about Clementine's gossip. When obviously I don't, though obviously you know I kind of do a bit. But only because I have a curious and marvellous brain.

I look down onto my page again so I can concentrate on listening and not looking. Then I hear the clip-clop of inappropriate-footwear-for-school patter past me whilst I'm tracing the peel, and Clementine and the terrible girls do that horrid laugh that immediately makes you feel like you're a fly that has got stuck up somebody's nostril and they are literally snorting you out. She shakes her head at me and lets her long legs walk her to the lunch room where she probably won't eat anything except gossip.

Chapter Six

I let a rottenous poisonous wash of regret leak into my head and begin beating myself up about all the times I've argued with my parents in front of Will. Moaned about them or complained or shouted at them or tried to run away from them, like a spoiled baby brat ghoul. And how he never made me feel bad or wrong or stupid. He just stood by me and let me do what I needed to do; he never judged me or made me feel awful. He just let me be me, when all along he never had a parent at all. Except his sister Annie. I mean, I know she's a bit bigger than us, but she takes care of Will every day; cleans his clothes, cooks for him, talks to him, understands him, drives him places, loves him. I guess she is his mum and dad and big sister all in one go. I can't imagine having to suddenly be a parent to Poppy and Hector – that would be a disgusting disaster. Wow, she truly is a hero.

I am walking out of school ready for home when I am nearly run over by the sprint of Maggie, who I know from the school magazine. She is currently 100% a witch, I gather, by all this black lipstick and nail varnish that she is wearing. But not one bit a terrifying witch, because it is impossible for her to not make a massive goofy smile all the time, even when she is delivering bad news, like now.

'Darcy!' she pants, completely out of breath. 'Can I borrow you for five minutes?'

'Of course,' I say, but in my brain I am thinking,

Borrow me? What am I? A vacuum cleaner? A whisk? A suitcase? You don't borrow a person, surely?

'What for?' I ask, as we wind our way back into the school and towards the music huts. This is where all the music lessons happen and Maggie, with her inky black fish lips, says, 'Do you know Clementine? An American girl? She's in your year.' And I say, 'Yes,' and manage to stop myself from also saying 'unfortunately' because you never know when people might be secret friends. Maggie nods and says, 'I thought so. Darcy, she's stolen Olly Supperidge as her new boyfriend off of Koala and Olly has dumped Koala!' And before I can react Maggie opens up the door to the main music hut where Koala (Nicola) who is the editor of the school magazine is sprawled out across the keys of the grand piano, sobbing.

Oh dear.

I can't help but be selfish about this a bit. Firstly, I hate being involved in stuff like this. This is for girly girl girls that want to talk about hairspray and diets and manicures, i.e. NOT ME. And secondly, I cannot imagine anything WORSE in the WHOLE ENTIRE WORLD THAT EVER BEED THAN OLLY SUPPERIDGE GOING OUT WITH CLEMENTINE! NOOOOOOOOOOOOOOOO-OOOOOO! This is a double-duo nightmare. My enemies, uniting! Nothing will ever be the same again. Ever.

Maggie nudges me, bursting me from my mind bubbles of fear. I shrug. What does she want me to do?

'Hi, Koala Nicola.' I step forward towards her. I flash back to when I first met Koala Nicola and she was this big growed-up editor and now she is a complete walrus sea lion snorting out a zombie gunge fountain.

'Darcy!' she bellows through big break-up tears that are the same size as gobstoppers. Crying over a boy? *Crying?* I can't believe this.

'Are you OK?' I ask gently.

'No. Do I look OK?' she hisses, slobbery, blub-bery, globbery snot and dribble pouring out of her eyes, nose, mouth.

'Is there anything I can do to make you feel better?' I ask timidly.

'YES!' She sniffles and wipes the tears from under her eyes. She looks like an absolute mighty moose-beast and it's tricky not to laugh. She breathes in and tries to focus on not fully transforming into a puddle of slime. Her eyes are red – it looks like she has been rubbing salt and lemons into them. 'You need to talk to Clementine and tell her that Olly is *not* a nice boyfriend.'

I sigh deeply. 'Koala, I don't know Clementine very well . . .'

'You *have* to. You have to tell her immediately so that she dumps him and then he will go back out with me!' Her face floods some more as she falls back across the piano, howling.

'Clementine hates me, she is never going to listen to me.'

'What about your friend Will? Can't you talk to him?' she splutters. 'Doesn't *he* fancy her? Can't he go out with her instead?' I don't know why but this annoys me so much. Just because her stupid Olly Supperidge has finally managed to go out with someone who is as disgusting as he is doesn't mean that my friends have to get dragged into this too.

'No. He does NOT fancy her, and anyway even if I WAS going to do that, WHICH I AM NOT, I couldn't anyway because Will isn't in school.'

'There must be *something* you can do.' Her eyes reach into mine, completely desperate and yearning.

I'm thinking, *Yeah, I could tell you to shut up and grow up and stop lowering yourself to crying and begging over such a waste.*

But I don't. Instead I say, 'Yes, I can help you with the magazine while you are having this crisis.' And then I say, 'Get yourself home, wrap up in a duvet and have some Maltesers.'

This actually works: Koala Nicola sits up and dries her eyes with her jumper. 'You're right. I should get home.' She sniffs and slides some more bogey syrup onto the cuff of her jumper.

'This piano will think it's at the bottom of the ocean if you cry into it any more, Koala Nicola,' I say, and then Koala Nicola laughs and I smile back, relieved to finally be able to let a grin go. The piano floats to the bottom of the ocean, crashing into the seabed with a clunk.

OLLY AND CLEMENTINE? Of all the villains in the history of villainy this has to be the worst. Oh no. NO. NO. NO. NO. NO. NO. NO.

At home, over peanut butter eaten straight out of the jar with a teaspoon, I talk to Mum about Will's dad coming to the school gates. She says I

probably shouldn't ring Will today because he hates me calling him on the phone at 'the best of times' so he won't want to speak on the phone tonight. Sometimes he pops by on his BMX after school and I look out of the window occasionally to see if he does, but there's no sign of him.

'Almost forgot!' Mum says, smiling. 'This came for you today, it's from Grandma, look at the handwriting.' She is right, I could recognize her handwriting anywhere, it's all loopy and shaky.

'What is it?' I'm shocked because it's not my birthday or anything. I begin to tear it open – it's that kind of brown envelope that if you rip it in the wrong place loads of fluff comes out of the packaging as if you've asked for a delivery of rabbit fur or the insides of a vacuum cleaner to be sent to your house. 'What about the others?' I ask, the *others* meaning Poppy and Hector. They will go mental if I have a present and they don't.

'She sent them sweets, don't worry.'

My face falls.

'AND before you moan, yes, you can have sweets too, don't panic.' Gosh, she knows me so well.

It's an ancient copy of the fairy tale *Sleeping Beauty*, all cracked and yellowing and smelling of dust and musk. The front cover is amazingly excellent. It's all old-fashioned with a beautiful sleeping woman with long blonde hair and flowers all around her. A note slips out onto my lap when I turn the book over.

Dear Darcy, I saw this in my local second-hand book shop, it is over one hundred years old and look who it's dedicated to . . . I just had to buy it.
    Enjoy, much love, Grandma.

One hundred years! Whoa, is that dinosaur time? I don't say this out loud in case it's not.

'Open it up,' Mum suggests, and inside is even loopier faded old writing from one hundred years before. It says:

Dear Darcy, on your birthday, Your Grandmother.

'WOW!' says Mum. 'What are the chances of that? Your grandma finding a book that's over one hundred years old dedicated to a you that's from *her* grandma? How amazing. You'll have to write and say a big Thank You.'

I am really chuffed with the book and I keep stroking it and touching it.

'Let's have a look then?' Mum lifts it up. 'I love that old book smell, isn't it wonderful? All that history, think about all the fingers that would have touched these pages, all the memories.'

I think about the Darcy this would have belonged to. *Who was she? What did she look like? Was she like me?*

And then Dad's key turns in the door and we hear him yell, 'Mum, kids, in the car!' Isn't it funny how Dad calls Mum 'Mum'? And Mum calls Dad 'Dad'? Like they are each other's parents. Children are not allowed to call parents by their first names because they get upset. I've got a girl in my class who does it, but she's a show-off.

'Where are we going?' I ask, laying the book down and putting my coat on. Perhaps this is going to be a spontaneous McDonald's trip, which would just be fantastic right now. A vegetarian-ish one. Of course.

'Don't ask questions!'

'This is silly, I've got a pie in the oven!' Mum complains. She has a little sprinkle of flour on her sleeve.

'Turn the oven off.'

'I was painting my nails pink!' Poppy shows her

hands to Dad – to be honest it is not a bad thing that Dad has interrupted this, she is not doing a good job.

'You can finish them when we get back, Pops.'

'I need a poo though,' Hector says, panicking a bit.

Dad releases a long-drawn-out breath. 'All right, quickly, everybody's got five minutes to run around and do what you need to do.'

And then, more like fifteen minutes later, we are all in the car.

'Now can you tell us where we're going?' Mum asks, peering round every corner and bend.

'We'll be there in two seconds.'

'Is it Disneyland?' Hector screeches.

'No, Hector, that's really far away,' Poppy says archly, blowing on her nails.

'How far?' Hector asks.

'Far,' I say.

'Fart?' questions Hector.

'If it's two seconds we should be here by now really,' Poppy remarks to Dad, all smug.

'Is it Fart away? In a kingdom Fart Fart away?'

'Sure, whatever, Hector. If you like,' I say, and then he does the biggest fart ever and it rumples the car seat and stinks like old cabbage and baby nappies. We all have to cover our noses with our jumpers.

'Here we are!' Dad pulls up outside a building full of enormous washing machines.

'The launderette?' Mum frowns.

'No! There! Look.'

I knewed exactly where he meant, it was Paws, Claws and Plenty More, the local pet shop, and outside of it chalked on a massive blackboard was this:

BRAND NEW LITTER OF KITTENS FOR SALE, TAKE 1 TODAY.

'There's only one thing that can cure a mouse problem and that's—'

'A fish!' Hector cries in joy and screams his way over to the door of the pet shop.

'A fish. Apparently.' Dad smirks, but Mum doesn't. She is likely thinking, *WHAT A TERRIBLY STUPID IDEA*. But Poppy and I can't help ourselves as we run after Hector to the window of the pet shop, squealing and commenting on everything we can drink in with our eyeballs.

The pet shop smells all sawdusty and dog-foody. There are lots of tins, pots and tubs and boxes of various toys to give to cats and dogs and rabbits and hamsters and gerbils, and mice too – if you like the mice you have in your house, not like us obviously. Then there are these big scary cardboard boxes with *POSTMAN LEGS* written on them and inside are huge mahoosive big bloody bones that make me feel a bit sick.

'Are they really postmen's legs?' I whisper-ask Mum.

'No, monkey.'

'MONKEY? MONKEY LEGS?' I yell.

'No, I was calling you "monkey". They probably belonged to some cows.'

I feel sick thinking about all the big cow legs in the box: I am such a good vegetarian. And then I remember that in the past few days I've eaten chicken curry and bolognese AND those pesky boot chicken nuggets and NOBODY reminded me. Oh great. I bet everybody thinks I am a weakling COWard with no principles or will power.

And that's when I look past the wall of rectangular mini swimming pools that are home to thousands of glittery tropical beautiful exotic fish. Past cage after cage of fluttery, squawky, gossipy birds nipping and napping in every shade of every colour, their posts covered in white sploshy bird poo like liquidated cloud. Past all of this are . . . the kittens.

There are eight in this litter, piled up on top of each other in a warm nest of snuggles and warmth, fluff and fur, like a nest of heated hair, a snuffly tumble of so much cuteness our eyes are set to explode.

Poppy, as usual, digs her hand straight in and pulls out a kitten with a big splodge over its eye.

'WAAAAAAHHHHH!' she squeals as she brings the podgy fluffball to her face and in baby language says, 'Ri rove ru, res Ri roo.' She then picks up another un-Poppy-proofed kitten in her other hand, a little black one, and confidently rolls the kitten up into her neck as if it's a violin and she's some kind of expert. She then begins muttering in baby language: 'Smoochie woochie toochie coochie noochie moochie oochie, boochie loochie froochie doochie smoochie boochie woochie.'

Which makes me feel sick, but actually not for long because then I see a little ginger one that looks just like Will. It makes me think about him, what's happening in his world right now. I stroke the ginger kitten's chin and he begins to purr, closing his eyes and relaxing his little body into mine. Mum and Dad have picked up a kitten each now too, and Hector is trying to hold the remaining three who are all purring but a bit crying too, he has a 50/50 success rate with animals.

We all begin arguing over our favourite one, using words like *my one* as if they already belong to us.

'Mine's got a lovely tail,' Hector tries.

'My one's got freckles on her nose,' Poppy adds.

'Mine's got a lovely, kind, thoughtful heart,' Hector suggests – he has been learning about *friendship* at school this week. Oh, those blissful days when you could do a WHOLE week on friendship.

'Oh, how can we choose?' Mum coos; she has truly been turned into a big gooey smitten kitten. But in one failing, falling horrendously awful swoop, our air balloon of kitten dreaming is punctured and sends us wailing to the ground.

'No, no, no,' says the little pet shop man with the bald head and the whiny voice like he's speaking with a clothes peg over his nose. 'I'm sorry, they are not for sale.'

'WHAT?' barks Mum. One thing you must know about mums is that they are actually roses made of barbed wire. They may look pretty and gentle but actually they are vicious and spiky, and if somebody messes with them all badness shall break loose.

The man steps back but isn't changing his mind. He is a tiny man, not much taller than me, and he begins to try and start 'shooing' us out. Obviously he has spent far too much time with dogs and not enough time with actual people to know you don't *shoo* my mum.

'Don't you DARE shoo me or my family!' My mum unleashes her alter ego, a wild, livid, powerful Angrosaurus rex with fire breath and yellow destroying eyes that could kill with a single glance.

'Remove yourself from the kittens, please.' He ushers us some more and then tries to protect the kittens from us as if we really are a family of monsters. 'These kittens have all been sold; I'm just waiting for them to be collected. Many apologies.' I hate it when people say they are sorry, but say it like they are reading words out of the newspaper, with no emotion and no heart, like a computer.

'Well, why on earth was th—' Dad tries, but the little man speaks over him, he is red now and cross.

'Are you stupid? The kittens are gone. Gone. Gone. Gone. Gone. Gone. Gone. Gone. GONE, and now I'd like YOU to do the same.'

In one moment the planets collide, the seas dry up, the planets drop from the sky and thunder and lightning and twisters and hurricanes and earth-quakes and tsunamis happen, and volcanoes begin erupting and the world is cracking as my mum opens her mouth . . .

'LISTEN, YOU **LITTLE** MAN, I DON'T KNOW WHO YOU THINK YOU ARE, SPEAKING TO MY FAMILY LIKE THAT. I DON'T KNOW WHO YOU THINK YOU ARE, OWNING A PET SHOP WITH THE CUSTOMER SERVICE OF A VOMIT-COVERED HOUSE FLY,

YOU NASTY LITTLE MAN. YOU HAD A SIGN UP OUTSIDE ADVERTISING KITTENS AND NOW YOU ARE SAYING YOU HAVE SOLD THEM ALL. EITHER YOU ARE TERRIBLY LAZY, OR YOU ARE TRYING TO BRING CUSTOMERS IN UNDER FALSE PRETENCES, USING THE BAIT OF BEAUTIFUL KITTENS TO LURE CUSTOMERS INTO YOUR RUBBISH **(insert lots of swear words)** SHOP. AND DON'T YOU WORRY – OF COURSE WE WILL BE LEAVING, LEAVING QUITE HAPPILY, AND I HOPE YOU KNOW YOU HAVE JUST LOST YOURSELF SOME REALLY EXCELLENT CUSTOMERS.'

The little man stands gawping. My dad evil-eyes him and goes a bit rude-boy gangster, like: '*Yo, that's my wife, that's my girl, y'all better recognize.*' And we follow her out like she's the big duck and we're all her little ducklings, waddling after her, livid and devastated (we really wanted those kittens) but we've got our mum's back.

As we get outside the shop and see the chalked sign advertising the kittens, Mum doesn't think twice – she picks the sign up and throws it in the nearest public dustbin and screams, 'LIES UPON LIES UPON LIES.' My mum can be quite dramatic, which is excellent.

We clamber into the car as quick as can be. Mum gets into the back, I think because that's where police officers put the criminals in their cars. I've seen it on TV so I know it's true and accurate. I get in the front, as I'm next after Mum in the food chain of shotgunning the passenger seat. Dad starts the engine as a man yells, 'Good work!' from across the road. 'I've always hated that pet shop idiot!' Mum covers her face and is shaking – I can see why she was adopted now. I reckon her real parents were a prehistoric mega-shark and a T-rex. It was an ill-fated romance that wasn't built to last.

'OK, where to now?' Dad says sarcastically.

'The pub,' Mum croaks.

Chapter Seven

A real-life thunderstorm starts later: a scary one that has a lot to say for itself and lights the sky up like a firework exploding. I have just finished writing my thank-you letter for Grandma, I'll show you what it says if you like:

Dear Grandma,

I probably would use your real name but I don't know what that is so I will stick to Grandma. Some people in my school call their grandmas 'Nan' or 'Nanna' or 'Granny' or 'Gran' or some have made up names too. It's funny that no matter which one in the world you choose you always stick with it and it becomes your new name, doesn't it? It never seems to amaze me when in a supermarket or park or whatever if I happen to shout out my mum's name, 'MUM!' which I mean OBVIOUSLY isn't her real name but it is for me, she will know that it is my voice calling her, she will know it's me. Even though there must be millions of mums all in the supermarket. Isn't that weird? And none of the other mums even look round, not even once, they all just go about their business as if I am invisible – but not in a mean way – even though I've shouted their name too. It's so special, isn't it? I guess I am just lucky that you are not deaded yet. Because lots of the kids in my school don't even have grandparents. So I am extra lucky.

I just wanted to say thank you lots for

my book, I love reading and fairy tales especially. Sometimes I wish there was more blood in fairy tales... Do you ever wish there was more blood in fairy tales? Please get back to me about that as soon as possible.

I hope you come to visit soon. If you do will you please bring us those delicious cherry buns that you make in the tin with the swans on? And Poppy says that when you give us money can you please make sure that the money is in coins and not a note because coins look like more and you can split it up into portions better whereas a note is just complicated.

Love you so much,

Darcy x x x

I feel bad. Poppy didn't even say that bit about the money but I had to get my point across without being rude. It is annoying getting notes, if you lose a note of money then it's gone for ever. And it doesn't even make a rattle noise like coins so it's tricky to find.

We are getting ready for bed, excited but tired after what feels like the longest day ever, when the phone rings unexpectedly.

'I'll get it!' I shout, and pick up Lamb-Beth for a cuddle before trudging over to the phone. She hates storms and her tail is all sad and facing downwards. I LOVE the thunder.

'Hello, Darcy, gosh you're up late.' It is patronizing Marnie Pincher. I roll my eyes and think about throwing the phone but perhaps we've all had enough drama for one day, what with the mice, Will and his dad,

Koala Nicola and Olly Supperidge breaking up, and my mum going nuts at the pet shop. 'Is Mum in?' She's not *your mum*, Marnie, *you* don't get to call her *Mum.*

'Yeah, let me get her. MUM! MUM! IT'S MARNIE.'

I hear Mum mumble a few hundred mean moaning things about Marnie under her breath, but when she gets on the phone it's all 'Heeeeeyyyy best friends'.

They aren't on the phone for long, and then I hear Mum and Dad chit-chatting for a bit, but it's hard to listen and crunch a biscuit at the same time. Then Mum rings Marnie right back, 'Yes, OK, thanks,' she says. 'Do bring it round.'

Bring WHAT round?

It's past our bedtime, but there is nobody telling us to go to bed and so we try to be really quiet and small so that Mum and Dad don't notice us. Maybe they will forget that we have a bedtime altogether? Fingers crossed.

The door knocks, and it's scary because the thunder crackles at the same time and the sky lights up making everything a white-silver colour. Dad opens the door and it's Marnie and her son Donald, both wearing rain macs and wellie boots. They are SO over the top.

Dad asks them both to come in for a hot drink but they say *no thanks* and *we can't stay* as *Donald needs to get to bed* because it's a *school night*. Then Marnie beadily glances at Poppy, Hector and me, and I can tell she is using every bit of discipline she can muster to not scream 'GO TO BED!' at us. Then Donald pulls out a cardboard box from under his rain mac. He gently (for him) passes it over to Dad, who has to use both hands to carry it.

'I didn't expect it to be this heavy,' he laughs awkwardly.

Marnie can't seem to get away quick enough, with lots of *come on then, love, let's get home* to Donald. The pair of them run out into the spidery rain, yelling, 'Bye,' whilst the sky continues shelling little globes of liquid diamonds all over them.

WHAT'S IN THE BOX?

WHAT'S IN THE BOX?

WHAT'S IN THE BOX?

We all settle down in the kitchen, Dad throwing Mum an anxious look. Hector is a terrifically impatient child, especially when he's tired like now.

'OP-EN IT,' he yells, patting the box.

'Hector!' Poppy snaps. 'Wait.'

'Kids . . .' Dad taps our hands off the box, which has started to rumble, juddering and vibrating. Hector leans back, as if the box is about to explode in our faces, and shields himself as Dad lifts the flaps open. A large grey head with pointy ears pops up like an oversized jack-in-the-box or the surfacing face of a livid hippo. Its eyes are a chalky green. The teeth are sharp and expression livid. It is one *moody* . . . . cat.

'She said he was a kitten, aged six to eight weeks!' Mum laughs through shock when she can just about get her words together.

'Ha! More like six to eight centuries,' Dad mutters, looking a bit cross.

But not as cross as this cat.

'All right, let's get him out.' Mum begins to tip the box a little, hoping the cat will gently slide out onto the kitchen floor, but the cat suddenly becomes like set cement and is incredibly heavy. 'Blooming thing weighs a ton.' She begins to get red in the face. 'We'll have to lift him out of the box.'

'How?' I can tell Dad does not want to touch this creature.

As Mum and Dad debate the best way to get the cat out, I suddenly remember Lamb-Beth. I haven't seen her since the door knocked. I jump up to look for her, and I know she will either be in one of our bedrooms, under the duvet, or in the living room under the coffee table. I check downstairs first, and there she is, as expected, curled underneath the table, shaking. I wonder if this fear is coming from more than just the storm outside.

'It's OK.' I stroke her fluffy head and her big eyes look back at me as if to say, *It's not really though, is it? You have brought a strange, angry beast into our home.* And I know she is right.

I hop back into the kitchen where everybody is staring at the cat and the box like they're the sword in the stone, impossible to separate them.

'OK ...' Dad breathes in. 'I'll just ... erm, let me just ...' He puts his hands into the box. 'I, erm ... he might have fleas!' Dad is really failing at being a superhero this week, what with the screaming at the sight of mice and letting himself be shouted at by the little man in the pet shop. The cat hisses furiously and Dad jumps back like he's seen a ghost.

'Let me get him.' Poppy leans forward, her hands go right under the cat's armpits and she lifts him up like a grumpy, chubby baby. 'Hello, tiger ...' she greets the cat, followed by, 'Wiger, liger, miger, biger, jiger ...' and then the cat hisses at her really loud and shows his claws and we all jump back

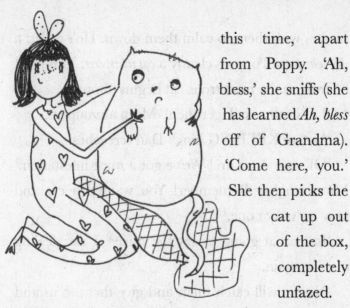

this time, apart from Poppy. 'Ah, bless,' she sniffs (she has learned *Ah, bless* off of Grandma). 'Come here, you.' She then picks the cat up out of the box, completely unfazed.

He is the biggest, fattest, most *solid* cat that I have ever seen. Poppy throws him over her shoulder, huffing and puffing under the cat's bulk, but he meekly lies there, while she pats his back like a baby being winded. 'There, there. It's OK now, you're safe here.'

HOW does she know what to do? I watched this programme once where this man runs around on TV visiting dogs all over America. Some of these dogs are really naughty or disobedient and he communicates with them to calm them down. He's called a *dog whisperer*. Poppy is clearly a *cat whisperer*. This must be true, as the monstrous cat begins to purr.

'Let's call him Tiger then!' Mum announces.

'Are we KEEPING him?' Dad screeches.

'Of course we are! We've got a mice infestation,' Mum laughs. 'Remember! You wanted a cat and now we've got one.'

'Is the cat going to eat the mice?' I ask, feeling queasy again.

'No, he will catch them and give them to us and we can put them in our cage.' This is Hector.

He is SO wrong.

'There is NO way that THAT cat is going to catch poor defenceless mice and then hand them to us INTACT without gobbling them up,' I screech.

'They aren't defenceless!' says Dad. 'You've seen 'em, Darcy, they are violent, vicious, vile rogues!'

Poppy is still cuddling the big dollop of cat. 'He doesn't want to be called Tiger,' she says.

'What does he want to be called?' I ask. I am both

impressed and jealous of Poppy. Why can't she just stop being good for one quick second and just be a bit rubbish?

'Hold on, let me ask.' She nestles into the cat's ear and does some whispering and then, like Dad does

when he pretends our teddy bears are talking to him (they always want us to go to bed for some reason, why did we get such moody party-killer teddies? I thought teddies were into picnics), she looks back at us and says, 'Pork. He would like to be called Pork.'

Hector laughs and Mum frowns, not convinced

that her daughter can speak full-blown *cat*. 'Are you sure he didn't say he would like to *eat* some pork?'

'Nope. He says a bowl of milk would be suitable but he would like to be called Pork.'

'That's settled then,' says Dad. 'Pork it is.' Dad then starts shaking his head as if he is saying *NO NO NO NO NO NO* over and over again. 'Two days ago I had a normal life,' he mutters, 'and now I seem to be living with a bunch of mice and a mangy cat.'

'Get over yourself,' Mum hisses, just like Pork. 'You never had a normal life.'

I think Dad might have wanted a cute new kitten that tumbled and got all caught up in rolls of wool and purred and hopped about. Not basically an angry dumpling, which is what we have, now Pork is here.

I scoop Lamb-Beth up and we make our way to bed. She is yawning and snuggling and mostly furious. Mum says animals don't always yawn because they are tired, they yawn because they are stressed too. It's when you need to get extra more oxygen to the brain.

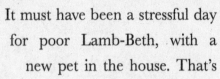

It must have been a stressful day for poor Lamb-Beth, with a new pet in the house. That's how I felt when Poppy was born, but you soon get used to it. You have to. I can't imagine Pork doing that much chasing and capturing or being that useful as he just sits there, like an oversized plop of furry grey mouldy mashed potato.

I think about Will and how his day must have gone. *What did his dad even say to him? What did his dad want? And how is Annie? What does she think about her dad returning?*

It's been a long day but I have lots of inspiration now, stuff to think about and write about. My head feels completely ready to burst but right now my eyes are sticking together and closing . . .

Chapter Eight

I can't even write the word *yawn* without
yawning. I can't even *read* the word *yawn*
without yawning. I can't even *say* the word
yawn without yawning. I can't hear it or see
it or say it now without yawning, and now
the word *yawn* doesn't even look like a word
any more. It's just a jumble of letters, an
organized pattern of shapes that mean nothing.
I bet you're yawning right now as you're
reading this, aren't you? Opening your mouth,
stretching your face, letting your jaw hang low,

your eyes water. The big vacuuming gust of tired used air that bellows out of your big gawping throat and makes your nostrils go all big like a fire-breathing dragon. Sometimes you release a groan to accompany the yawn, a big wail-like whale song. Sometimes it's silent. I bet you're yawning now, my friend. I bet you are.

I put my pen down. If that doesn't count as 'persuasive writing', I don't know what will. I think Mr Yates will be pleasantly surprised. Persuasive writing is what you do when you are trying to convince someone to do something, and I think I've just nailed it. I do a bit more yawning myself as I feel like I've got one trapped at the back of my throat.

'Boring you, is it, Darcy?' Mr Yates asks.

'No, I'm just tired,' I say. Everybody looks up and the sound of pens scratching and squiggling grinds to a halt. 'We got a tramp cat last night,' I announce to the class. Some kids snort and laugh a bit.

'How very nice for you.' Mr Yates nods. 'Thank you for sharing.' Most people would accept this as conversation over, but not me.

'He is called Pork,' I continue, as some more of my classmates giggle and swivel round to face me, 'but we didn't choose that name, *he* did – he told my sister Poppy in a whisper that this is what he would really like his name to be. We had to listen and let him have his wish because he is to be a mouse-catcher for us – we have mice eating all our things, even Mum's moisturizer. Dad bought a big tub, a bucket almost, of bright blue poison pasta to murder the mice but it didn't even work. Much to his disappointment, as Dad's really *into* murdering mice. Then we went to the pet shop and stroked loads of tiny kittens but then Mum went absolutely mental at the man because he was a swear word, and so we had to go to the pub and get Mum a bit drunk. Then the thunder and lightning came and our parents' friends, who we all hate a bit, rang us up and said they found a stray tramp cat and did we want to have him as a mouse-catcher and . . . well . . . that's Pork.' I cough a bit, and then I do a big yawn. One by one, including Mr Yates, everybody yawns back. Like a mirror.

'Thank you for that interesting and imaginative adventure of yours, Darcy. I think we were all entertained,' Mr Yates says after his yawn, his hand curled in front of his mouth like a protective paw.

Even though he is being sarcastic I still say, 'You're welcome,' and do a bow. Everybody laughs.

'As much as we would all love to have a little nap now on our desks, we've still got work to do. Everybody back to work, finish our persuasive writing.' I don't know why teachers use words like 'our', as it's not like *they* have to do it! 'And if you're finished . . .' – this applies to me – 'you can catch up on some reading or you can work on some creative writing in your exercise book.'

I've got the copy of *Sleeping Beauty* in my bag, the one Grandma gave me. I take it out and flick through it. The pictures are so beautiful and look like somebody worked really extra hard on them. I touch them with my hands. I pretend my finger is a paintbrush and go all around the outside of the lines with it. That same musty, dusty, musky, dusky smell powders all over my desk in clouds and some of my classmates look at me disgusted for bringing an old book into school. But I think they are disgusting for not respecting my old book.

After reading a bit more I feel inspired – it makes me want to write a story of my own. So I do, because writing is like catching a fish, you always have to have

your net at the ready. I want to write my very own
Sleeping Beauty, a fairy tale to read before bed.

The King was tired. He
had not slept for weeks.
He had not slept for
weeks because he had
so many important kingly
worries inside his great
kingly head, worries
about money and war
and the weather. Really
grown-up worries. He
knew he was tired
because his eyes had
big grey browning circles underneath them, like
somebody had rested two cups of coffee over
them. He was clumsy too – he would bump
and crash into things and he was so grouchy
and grumpy and whenever anybody said, 'Don't
mind the King, he's just tired,' he would snap

143

at them like a yappy dog and shout, 'I AM NOT TIRED!' But he was. Everybody knew that.

The Queen was very distressed. She missed the days when her husband was playful and fun. He used to love driving around in his posh cars and playing tennis on the lawn. He loved swimming and long walks and hosting elaborate dinner parties, but since his sleep had vanished, so had much of his love for life. They had tried everything: they got a choir in to sing him lullabies, and they got a herd of real sheep in for him to count, but nothing seemed to do the trick. Until late one night, during a crackling evening of thunder and lightning, there was a knock at the door of the palace.

Knock. Knock. Knock.

The Queen was wrapped up in a blissful blanket of slumber and did not hear the door, but the wide-awake King did. His guards asked if the door should be opened and the King nodded.

'I am so bored anyway, in my bed doing nothing except staring at the ceiling, and even if it is a baddie I would welcome their attempts at badness as entertainment.'

He sat up from his bed and his body creaked and cracked like the snapping of celery hearts. He reached for his red velvet robe and tied the golden tassels up around his waist and then he scratched his beard. What visitor would come at this unearthly hour, in the pouring rain?

I'll tell you who. The door opened, all guards standing to attention, their weapons at the ready.

'Please,' said the lady who was standing there. 'I mean no harm.'

'It's a gypsy!' said one of the guards.

'Silence!' ordered the King. He actually wanted to know the exact same thing, but

as he was in charge here it had to be HIM
to ask the question. 'Are you a gypsy?'

'I roam and travel like a gypsy but I am
a healer and I have come because you, your
Royal Highness, need healing, and I wish to
be of service to you.' The lady got down on
one knee. It was now, with her head bowed,
that the King got a good chance to survey
the woman. She had long knotty black
hair and was covered in some of the most
astonishing jewels; his
wife would die for
some of them. They
twinkled and shone
under the dazzling
brilliance of the
lightning from outside.

Although she was drenched from rainwater, the sheen of the water gave her a magical sparkle and strength that made her seem almost mythical. The wet also made her look vulnerable, like a child or small animal. She had to come in, for tea at the very least.

'You may stand,' he said, and she did. 'How are you proposing to heal me?'

'I know you are sleep-deprived. A king needs his sleep like any woman or man, but your sleep is particularly precious. You have extra-large decisions to make as a king and it is crucial you are not too tired.' The woman spoke calmly and did not mind the wind or rain as it rumbled through her hair, ripping the knots in her hair apart. The King almost fell into her words like a warm bath.

'Prepare tea and food, clean clothes and a bed for . . .'

'Pens down, class, nice work,' Mr Yates says, and the bell rings, meaning it is lunch time. I look around at all my classmates; surely one of them will come over and congratulate me for sharing my Pork story in class, or ask me if I want to walk around the field together. Or something. But no. Everybody walks past me and all I can do is pretend to rub some ink off my hand that wasn't even really there and feel angry at Will for not being at school and leaving me to fend for myself.

This is the second day that Will hasn't been in. I can't think of anything to do, so I decide to go and see Mavis in Reception. Even if she has no good news about Will she might have shortbread and would certainly have that gorgeous Scottish voice to soothe me with. The moment I leave Mr Yates's classroom I see Koala Nicola in the hallway, bawling her eyes out and being consoled by a couple of older girls in her year, and so I quickly sneak back into my classroom until they pass. I cannot be dealing with her drama right now. I slip up against the wall like a

shadow and hold my breath. Her howls snake down the corridor, heavy and deep and heartbroken. Yuck. I get down the stairs towards Reception and out of absolutely nowhere I hear a horribly recognizable voice say:

'Wassup?'

Which is a phrase I never know how to reply to. It's Olly Supperidge, obviously exercising his newly-learned-from-Clementine Americanisms.

'Erm. I'm just going to see Mavis at Reception.'

'Why? She's so annoying!' Olly says, smirking.

'I don't think she is actually.' I feel like defending Mavis.

'She's like really nosy.'

'Nosy?'

'Yeah. *Well* irritating. My dad calls people like her a sticky beak.'

'A sticky beak?' I ask, as a picture pops into my head of Mavis with a big beak with loads of glue and fluff attached to it, squawking in a Scottish accent.

'Yeah, sticky beak means nosy parker. That's what Mavis is.'

'I like her,' I say defiantly.

'You would. Anyway, how's your writing coming along?'

'Erm. Fine, I guess. Why?'

'Think you'll have some stuff for us at the school mag to read soon?'

I am not really sure how to answer that. Us? Who does he mean by US? Please don't tell me Clementine is involved in the school magazine now? 'Er . . .' I start.

'Get cracking then, Burdock, bucko, we really want to publish a great story by you in this edition.' I see he *still* hasn't managed to stop speaking like a 1930s boy at a posh boarding school.

'OK . . .' I say.

'Less time with Granny Mavis then! Ha! More time writing?' Olly smirks, and this really annoys me. Don't tell *me* what to do! How about less time being such a wretched disease, Olly Supperidge – how about that, eh?

'I'll write at home,' I say, mostly to make him leave me alone. I could already see the clock chewing up the minutes in lunch break which always ticks by fast anyway. Weird, because the rest of the day runs at a tortoise pace.

'Great. Well, catch you later.' He waves and slopes off.

'See ya.'

YA? *YA?* Did I really just say *ya*? Oh, help me. I hate him even more now that he was nasty about Mavis. If it weren't for Mavis I would never have got to sit backstage in the Reception desk area. I am a true VIP because of that. I am starting to realize that without Will I don't really have too many friends at school . . . hmmm.

'Hello, Mavis,' I say as I go up to her desk. She moves the glass shutter back and her face lifts.

'Bad thunder and lightning last night, wasn't it?'

'Really bad.'

'Were you scared?'

'No, not really, I quite like it.'

'You're braver than me then!' She chuckles

warmly. *How dare Olly say Mavis isn't lovely?*

'Have you heard from Will or his sister Annie?' I ask. My finger is drawing shapes on the wall.

'I only heard from his sister Annie to say he won't be in today. But that's all, I'm afraid. Perhaps give him a call when you get home this evening?'

My heart sinks slowly to my stomach. I feel absolutely friendless like an only lonely child with nobody to talk to. Why did I have to put all my eggs in one friendship basket?

'Thanks.' I slowly walk away. *What do I do with myself now?*

'Darcy?' Mavis calls, her face shining brightly. 'Go and get yourself a wee sarnie and you can come and eat your lunch back here, with me.'

'Are you sure?' I ask.

'Positive.'

The idea of spending lunch in the warm cosy hutch of Mavis's desk is appealing and something that cheers me up. The idea of a wee sandwich not so much. Oh yes, she means LITTLE, remember.

I choose a cheese and pickle sandwich on brown bread; just because I've eaten meat a couple of times doesn't mean I can go around doing it constantly. I choose brown bread because it's healthier than white bread, and white bread is for when you're sick or when you've had to do your shopping at the news-agent. Also I just want to show off to Mavis and look like I pick brown bread out of choice.

We don't talk much because Mavis says she doesn't really get a lunch break and has lots of work to do, but I sit and eat my sandwich and get back to writing my story. I see Will's school bag in the corner, all crumpled like a sack of potatoes that have gone off. It looks so pathetic without him.

'What's that?' Mavis asks. *Uh-oh, maybe this is the beginning of her sticky beaking. I hope not.*

'A story I'm writing.'

'Wow, what happens?' she asks.

'I don't know yet. I never know – that's why I like to write because I never know what's going to happen next.'

'Wonderful. I don't know how you do it! Ah, I am in *awe* of writers. Creativity is such a special thing.' There is a strong difference between nosiness and showing an interest, why can't people see that?

'What does "*orrr*" mean, Mavis? Is it a Scottish word?'

'I don't think so; it's like to have respect for something or somebody, admiration . . . to look *up* to. Different to *oar* spelled O A R, which is for boats.'

'Oh yes, like paddles.'

'Exactly. This awe is spelled A W E.'

'Got it.'

'So one of your characters might be *in awe* of another.'

'Not at the moment, but maybe, if I choose. At the moment this strange sleep healer lady has just knocked on the front door of the King's palace.'

155

'Ah!' Mavis laughs, and her grandma-like boobies bounce. 'What an imagination. A sleep healer! I need one of those for all the snoring my husband does, he wakes me up every night!'

I laugh.

'What's her name? This sleep healer?'

'I don't know actually. I want her to have a magical name, something unusual and not obvious.'

'Hmm . . . let's see . . .' Mavis starts fiddling with her computer. 'Maybe I could type in the search bar . . . sleep fairy . . . let's see if any names come up when I search that . . .'

'Or goddess . . . is there a sleep god?'

'Good idea.' Mavis nods. Some of the other staff in the room are huffing and tutting and sighing at their desks and furiously eating their silly Lamb-Beth lunches of salad and carrot sticks.

'Here we go, look at this. Morpheus.'

I look at the screen and see a very artistic and naked illustration of a god, and I briskly get a bit shy and blushy.

'He looks handsome,' Mavis adds.

'Yuck, it's a painting. You can't have a crush on a painting.' I poke my tongue out in disgust.

'Oh, shush you; I can have a blimmin' crush on a slice of cheesecake if I want to. Speaking of which, pass the shortbread, will you? Top drawer.' I reach for the shortbread in its tartan tin. She takes the lid off and it's clear that since yesterday, a LOT of it has been devoured. 'What?' Mavis looks at me blankly as she catches my jaw drop at the nearly empty tin. 'These hips don't grow themselves!'

We laugh, and she begins to crunch on the short-bread. I make sure to take one for after lunch before she devours them all. 'The thing is, your character is a woman, so why don't you call her . . . say . . . ooo . . . *Morphina*?'

'Morphina?' I say out loud, nibbling on the sandwich crust. Morphina. I like that. 'Yes. I like that. I'll call her Morphina.'

'See.' Mavis slurps on her tea. 'Knew there was a reason we had to have lunch together.'

'Morphina.' The lady smiled and said, 'My name is Morphina.'

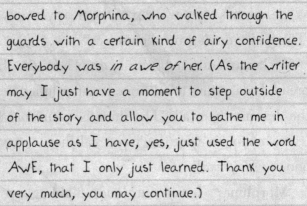

And the King welcomed her into his palace; the guards loosened their grip on their weapons and bowed to Morphina, who walked through the guards with a certain kind of airy confidence. Everybody was *in awe of* her. (As the writer may I just have a moment to step outside of the story and allow you to bathe me in applause as I have, yes, just used the word AWE, that I only just learned. Thank you very much, you may continue.)

Morphina was given a beautiful room in the tall tower; she could stay there for as long as it took to get the King to sleep easily. For now she would dry off and have lemon tea,

shortbread and a cheese and pickle sandwich
on brown bread, because it was healthier.
First thing in the morning, she and the King
would begin the healing process. (As the writer
may I just step outside of the story for a
brief moment to ask the opinion/advice of the
reader? Do you think I will have to credit
Mavis for suggesting this new word AWE to
me? I mean, will she want recognition or do
you think she will let this one slide? I can't
really pass it off as my own now, can I?
This is awkward. I think I might just go with
it, have confidence and use it and if she raises
it with me thank her politely. Ok, as you were.)

The Queen woke bright and early
to find her husband slumped in a
chair in the Great Hall, like he
had been shot through the
heart.

'My LOVE!' She ran
over to the chair where

her husband gently sat up, a bit dazed. 'Sorry, it's just that I woke and you weren't in the bed and then I see you here like this . . . I thought the worst . . .'

'It's OK, my Queen, please. We have a guest – this is Morphina.' The Queen immediately jumped up and brushed down her nightdress and tried to pat her sleepy hair into place.

Morphina looked very beautiful today now that she was refreshed and dry and her jewellery blinked one hundred times over.

'I beg your pardon, I wasn't expecting a guest, how do you do?' said the Queen.

'I am very pleased to meet you, Your Majesty, but if you don't mind, your husband and I have work to do.'

The Queen was quite taken aback. She looked to her husband, who would never stand for this insolence usually. But he shrugged and said, 'There *is* much work to be done.'

The Queen's nose had been quite put out of joint, but she nodded and said something posh like, 'I bid thee farewell.'

As she stalked off, she felt very irritated. She couldn't stop thinking about Morphina's natural beauty and her effortlessly charming fairy-ish knotty hair. If the Queen didn't bother to brush her hair, then the kingdom would gossip and make fun of her! And where did this newcomer get all that beautiful jewellery from too, eh?

That night the King did not sleep. The Queen woke the next day in an ugly mood. She thought about the day before and how she had to spend all day in her parlour, alone, reading books and stitching and drinking so much tea she was constantly weeing, and all this for her husband to have yet ANOTHER sleepless night. She just didn't trust this Morphina and her silly ideas. Still, the Queen went down to the Great Hall to see her

husband having
breakfast with
Morphina. She was
NOT happy.

'Ah, smoked salmon, I see?'

'It's delicious,' said the King. 'Wild Alaskan.'

'You should sit with us,' Morphina said, as
though this was *her* table.

The Queen slit her eyes as if Morphina was
the bright sunshine. 'Morphina, did you know my
husband yet again endured a sleepless night?'

'I did.' Morphina slurped her grapefruit juice
quite calmly and patted her lips with the napkin.

'Well, aren't you *supposed* to be *healing*
him?'

'I am.'

162

'Well, get to it!' the Queen snapped.

'You have a very supportive wife, your Royal Highness,' Morphina said with heavy sarcasm as she got up from the table. 'I have to work now, thank you for breakfast.'

'Where shall I meet you later?' the King called after her, but Morphina, without saying a word, exited the Great Hall, leaving only her footsteps to do the talking as they clicked over the floor, echoing off every wall.

The King threw his head into his hands. 'Why did you say that?' he asked his wife angrily. 'Now you've upset her she's never going to help me sleep.'

'Well, I think she's a fraud, a waste of time.'

'You don't like the fact she has beautiful jewellery more like!' the King bellowed.

'How could she afford all that anyway?'

'Perhaps they were presents? From other tired kings and queens, to say thank you. Perhaps

I'm not the only person she's healed?'

'Healed!? You didn't sleep a wink last night.'

They sat in silence, picking at the smoked salmon.

Suddenly the doors to the Great Hall reopened and the entire staff of the palace entered, from the guardsmen and guardswomen to the seamstresses and court jester.

'What is all this?' cried the King.

Morphina walked towards him. 'I need to work with your staff today, as they are a vital piece in the puzzle to ensure you get your rest.'

'How?' the King demanded. His Queen rolled her eyes; this was becoming a saga now!

'You shall see, please let me work.' Her jewellery sent reflected light flying across the hall like mirror balls, blinding the King and Queen, who reluctantly got up and left the hall.

The King paced up and down in his drawing room whilst his wife watched some

TV. He couldn't relax. 'What's going on?' he boomed. 'They've been ages.'

'I'm not getting involved,' the Queen tutted. 'Pass the cookies.'

'That's ALL my staff, EVERYBODY she's got in there! All in one room, even my gardener. The cooks — my guards! What if an enemy were to attack?' The more he thought about it, the more it angered him, but just when the King was about to smash something up in pure sleep-deprived anger and frustration, Morphina knocked on the drawing-room door.

'We're ready for you now, your Royal Highness.'

'At last!' the King said, breathing deep. 'Wife, come on.'

'I don't want to be a part of this, thank you very much. I sleep just fine,' said the Queen snarkily.

'Come. On.'

'No. I told you I didn't trust her, I told

you I didn't like her, I didn't want her here
in the first place, it was you that let her in
and so you have to do this on your own!'

'Very well. Thanks so much for your
support,' the King groaned in sarcastic suffering.
'All the late nights I've had to face, look at
the bags under my eyes – they are big enough
to carry all the new clothes that I'll buy you
when I take you shopping tomorrow after I've
had a LOVELY NIGHT'S SLEEP!'

'Don't you bribe me,' his wife muttered,
reaching for a fourth cookie.

'Wife, please. My Queen?'

'I don't trust her.'

'Please? For me? I'm begging you.' And
that must have worked as the Queen got up
and followed her husband to the door, where
Morphina calmly led them towards the Great
Hall, parading about as if this palace belonged
to her and she was taking some tourists on
a tour.

Inside the Great Hall were all the staff, all lined up in rows, like mini-queues for the post office. And in the middle of the room was a great big beautifully made bed,

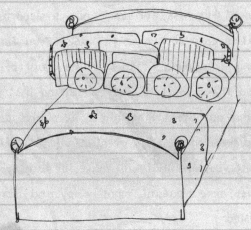

a bed so big and so grand and inviting with soft goose-feathered pillows, a gold-laced quilt and big silk throwovers. The sort of bed you would want to get into and never leave.

Morphina asked the King to stand before the bed, facing his staff. The Queen was still not convinced and hung back close to the door, in case she got bored of this and needed to escape for more cookies or an episode of *The Simpsons*.

'Thank you, everybody, for supporting his Royal Highness, for promoting his sleep and taking care of him as he has of you for so long,' Morphina began. 'On the count of three, you know what to do – something that will surge our Great King into a deep and restful slumber, one that is overdue, one that he deserves, one that will make, in turn, your lives more pleasant, more happy and more rested.'

This was already annoying the Queen. She hated this Morphina. What did *she* know? She quietly crept out of the Great Hall and sneakily got away. She knew her husband would be very let down and sad if he were to see her leave, as this was important to him. But what a load of old codswallop!

Back in the hall, the King was very excited.

He felt like he had waited centuries for this sleep and he felt very proud when he saw all his staff staring back at him, ready to serve him. It made him feel strong and robust, ready for almost anything. How fortunate he was to have Morphina stumble across his home that wet evening like that.

Meanwhile, the Queen had poured herself a lovely refreshing cup of tea and had raided the snack pantry. She felt so lucky to have the whole kitchen to herself without the chef or the maids snooping around spying on her or her dressmaker judging her for eating another one of her beloved cookies. But then it suddenly occurred to her. *She could have a look, couldn't she? In Morphina's bedroom?* She could find out who she really was and prove to her husband that she was no good! A fraud! A liar! Ha!

So up she crept, step by step, step by step. It was so weird and unordinary for her to have her whole vast palace at her feet, as it was usually so big and grand and full of noise and clatter and movement. But now it felt even bigger and grander and so empty, like a museum at night. She felt like a burglar, mazing her way around her own home like an intruder. Her own footsteps made her jump, and every sound was almost amplified, like a speaker erupting next to her ear. Eventually she reached the door of the guest room where Morphina was staying, and although she knew it was bad behaviour she gently twisted the brass knob and let herself in.

There didn't seem to be anything unusual here. Just a few clothes and a couple of books . . . but then . . . the Queen spotted a shine with her magpie eye, a shine from the corner of the room, a blinding shine.

It was jewellery. Some of the most beautiful jewellery she had ever seen.

How did Morphina have all this? And just

to carry it around too, as if it was no big deal? The Queen lifted the jewels out of their case. A shooting emerald green took her right back to being small again and tasting jelly for the first time; the jiggles it gave her reminded her of the river where she used to play when she was small. Lost in the boggy foggy marshes, collecting frogspawn, and the smell of mud. Or the sapphire on this necklace sailed her to the ocean, letting her take a deep breath and dunk her head into the deep. She felt like a kite, whirling in the clean clear blue sky. This blue was like the eyes of a child with a balloon. The crystals, as untarnished and untouched as pure frozen new ice . . . every angle was perfection.

The jewels melted into her own hands, her fingers on the silver and gold and cold platinum, like holding a sword or a weapon or something even more powerful: like holding a planet.

And when she spun the jewellery around to see the date, the carat, the maker, this is what she saw . . .

HER MAJESTY QUEEN TRUDY
TO MY BELOVED QUEEN SAKI ON YOUR BIRTHDAY
PRESENTED TO QUEEN MARSHA ON HER JUBILEE

And on the next and next and next piece, new names, new dates, new messages and none, not a single one, said 'Morphina'. These were treasured items that had belonged to royalty.

Morphina was not a healer. Morphina was a *thief*.

Downstairs, Morphina was standing with her hands on her hips, and commanding the staff of the palace to yawn. 'In three, two, one . . . YAWN . . .' and in unison they yawned one ginormous mighty yawn, a yawn so mammoth it caused them to all nearly snap their necks off. It was volcanic, like an engine, like an earthquake and every single person in the room (except for Morphina) dropped to the floor to sleep. Even the King was snoring, finally, like an exhausted bulldog.

'Yawning, the most contagious disease of all!' Morphina sighed as she looked at the sleepy heads. 'Now let's get to *real* work!' she growled and headed upstairs.

The Queen heard the noise of the yawn even from the tower, and it frightened her. Was her husband OK? She decided to scoop up all the jewellery into her pockets and make a grand entrance to the Great Hall – she would expose that woman as a thief in front of everybody!

Morphina was moving around the palace briskly, as if browsing in an antique shop. She took her time, pinching golden goblets, shields and silver.

The Queen, making her way down the stairs, had a bird's-eye view of that little dark-haired burglar. She could see her rummaging and snooping.

'Ah, doing your work, I see, as you promised. But I didn't realize it was so *dirty*.'

Morphina was shocked and embarrassed, but was too well practised as an arch-criminal to crumble.

'I like to make myself useful, pay my keep, do my bit whilst staying somewhere. I'm only tidying!' Morphina cracked a smile but it was as broken as a dinner plate on a marble floor.

The Queen continued to walk down the staircase, her eyes fixed on Morphina. 'Tidying these away into your suitcase perhaps?' She lifted up one of the many jewels she had found in Morphina's bedroom.

'That's MINE!' Morphina snarled and stepped towards the Queen. 'You stole that from me!'

'And you stole from queens around the world! Now where's the King?'

'Sleeping,' Morphina replied and waited, as if on a chessboard, for the Queen to make her next move.

'And was Trudy's husband asleep when

you took her necklace? What about Saki's? Marsha's? Were they all cuddled up with their teddy bears, leaving you to strip their jewellery boxes bare?'

Morphina knew she'd been caught out and there was nothing more she could do so . . .

'There goes the dreaded bell, I'm afraid, hen.' Mavis is genuinely looking disappointed that I have to stop writing and leave. 'Did you get some good writing done? I don't know how you do it, sit there and just write like that. Doesn't your mind wander off?'

'Of course, but that's why I like it. I do it so my mind *can* wander off.'

'Well, you must be Wander Woman . . .' Mavis laughs, then she wipes her eyes with her finger. I laugh too, collecting my things.

'Work on your story tomorrow, and will you

read it to me tomorrow lunch time?'

'Course I will.' I wave goodbye, even to the moody other ladies eating their boring diet lunches and I realize that hanging out with Mavis at lunch time is not bad at all.

Chapter Nine

'AHHHHHHH! Darcy! Darcy! Quick!' It's Poppy, of course, making a racket as usual. 'GET YOUR FAT BUM IN HERE NOW!' She is so excited her voice sounds like it's climbing up a mountain.

It's really special to be greeted in this way by an overexcited sister but I'm feeling that horrid thing where you're not entirely sure whether you want to be fun right now. Perhaps I just want to wallow and be a lump of grump.

'DARCY! DARCY!' she calls again. I kick my dompy shoes off and they hit the ground like a boulder dropping onto tarmac. I follow the sounds of Hector and Timothy's (Poppy's tutu-wearing ballerina best friend) laughter to the living room. Pork is sitting in a pink babygro and bonnet, in a pram, purring.

'Poppy! You can't do that, that's naughty,' I say and go right over to Pork to undress him.

'No, he hisses if you take him out of it, he likes it. He TOLD me.' Poppy is missing a few teeth at the moment and it's making her look like she is a boxer after a big fight, or possibly a grandma and so you can't really take her seriously.

'Honestly,' she says. 'He actually chose the outfit. He went over to the doll wearing this babygro and pointed at it and whispered, *I want to look like that.* He picked it out, like how Mum does with the models in magazines.'

It's hard to digest, but Poppy *is* the cat whisperer, after all. Pork is purring and Timothy is snapping away furiously with his posh camera, taking photographs of Pork. 'I want to put this online, could you imagine? He will be a viral sensation overnight!'

'He does love it,' Hector adds, and takes out a packet of fruit pastilles from his pocket.

'Oi!' I bark, holding my hand out. 'Pay the tax woman.' He huffs but he knows he has to pay up and unwraps the top. The next one in line is a yellow one. He grins a bit and places the little sugar sunshine in my palm. I shake my head. 'I don't think so . . . do you?' He sighs again and eats the yellow one. Next in line is a green one. I cough and pretend to be dis-interested, my patience is being tested. He puts that one on the side for later and then winds the packet down again until a ruby-red glittery sugar-covered pellet of goo shows its face and OBVIOUSLY this is the chosen one for me.

Dad is in the kitchen doing some accounts on his laptop and Lamb-Beth is sprawled across his lap. 'Hi, Dad.' I kiss him on the cheek.

'Hi, poodle.' He smiles, then looks at Lamb-Beth. 'We're protesting, aren't we?' Lamb-Beth opens one eye from her snoozing and grunts in my face.

'About Pork?'

Dad nods. 'All the slobby thing does is sleep and eat and stare. I was trimming my beard in the bathroom mirror this morning and got the fright of my life to see 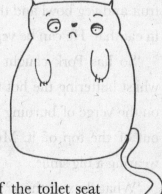 Pork propped up on top of the toilet seat glaring at me, right in the face, with that miserable frown.'

I laugh and go to the toaster. It really is Marmite-on-toast time now. I make some for Poppy, Timothy, Hector, Dad and even Lamb-Beth too. Mum doesn't want any, because toast is 'too addictive', she says. She is too busy upstairs anyway, rolling Hector's socks into balls. She does have a point. I could bathe in Marmite. In our house we ALL love Marmite.

I think about giving Pork some ham, because all cats like ham, but then there's a battle going on in my head that it feels weird giving something called Pork some ham. I see an old tired mushroom in the fruit and veg bowl and think I might see if he wants to eat that. He can be veggie like me.

'So has Pork caught any mice yet?' I ask Dad whilst buttering the hot toast. I like my toast nearly on the verge of burning so that the Marmite steams out of the top of it. Mum comes into the kitchen wearing a big smile.

'What do you think?' Dad mutters with sarcasm and rubs his head with his hands. Mum begins to chop carrots. The tops of them sit like little gentleman heads wearing top hats.

'Have you seen Hector?' she whispers.

'Why?'

'Timothy and Poppy have dressed him up as a princess!' Mum snorts, which she always does when she is trying not to laugh.

I shriek in excitement. I can't *wait* to see this. I grab the plate of toast off the side and run in to see Hector AND Timothy dressed as princesses with

Poppy pretending to scrub their feet and fan them. Pork is still in the pram. Hector for a second looks at me a bit like I have let him down, and freezes as if he's been caught out, but I throw him a massive reassuring smile. I am NEVER letting him forget this one.

'Darcy, meet our servant!' Timothy is delighted with himself.

'Yes, I am the servant and these are the mean princess sisters,' Poppy adds. Never have I seen such a happy servant. She is beaming cheek to

183

cheek. Poppy does more scrubbing and fanning, and then pretends to *shhhh* the baby (Pork). I am laughing really hard now. Wish Will was here to see this.

'I've got toast here, it's hot.'

'I don't eat bread,' Timothy mutters. 'It's utter sewage for the physique. I only eat sushi and fruit and green tea.' We all look at him absolutely shocked. 'As if!' he cracks up, rolling around, and then his face pours into a smile. 'Darling please.' Relieved, I leave the plate with them and go to eat my toast in the kitchen.

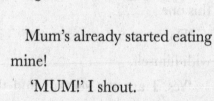

Mum's already started eating mine!

'MUM!' I shout.

'Oh, yum!' She licks her lips; she looks about five years old.

'Here!' I'm angry and slam the lid of the Marmite onto the jar. 'HAVE it.'

I decide to ring Will. I know his number off by heart but I still pretend to look it up on the little laminated sheet that Mum made that has all our important phone numbers on it.

It rings. And rings. And rings. I can hear the wails of laughter from Timothy and Poppy from the other room. And then Annie's voice comes onto the phone:

'It's Annie and Will,
Leave a message after the beep
And one of us will remind the other one
To call you back but most probably will just forget.
Thanks.
Oh, unless you're Chad, then STOP calling.
Byeeeeeeee.'

Then there's loads of really loud giggling from both Annie and Will – it's that kind of laughter where you can't get your breath back, and it makes me laugh too just listening to it. Then it hangs up. Chad is Annie's ex-boyfriend who it is illegal not to hate. And I don't like breaking the law.

I don't leave a message.

When I put the (Marmite fingerprinted) phone down, I see Mum in the reflection of the mirror. 'No answer?' she asks softly, and I shake my head. 'Try again later?'

Pork is now out of his babywear. Dad said he thought it was 'humiliating for the cat'. Apparently 'cats are very proud'. But to be honest I think he just wanted to ruin everybody's fun because he wasn't dressed up as a princess too.

Then Dad leaves for football, which he plays in the park with loads of other dads who are all a bit slow and chubby and bald. We wave him off and he acts like he is off to climb a mountain, so dramatic.

Poppy says Pork was prob-
ably a prince or some kind
of 'Royal Child' in
another life and so
has to be treated like
one. She feeds him
slightly warmed milk
in a teacup. Lamb-
Beth rolls her eyes at
this. Poppy then reports
that Pork said he
would be really
cross at her if
she didn't get to invite her friends over for a sleep-
over as he's *desperate* to meet them all. She also said
he fancied a Chinese takeaway for dinner tomorrow
night. He didn't actually say those things, did he?
And both Lamb-Beth and I know it. We are on
to her.

Later we eat Mum's chicken stew and carrots and
Mum says, 'Why not invite Will over tomorrow? I'm

sure he will be back in school then.'
Dad's home now and is soaking his
feet after football in the washing-
up bowl AGAIN. He is really
sweaty, but Mum says it's good
for Dad to 'let off some steam'.
As if Dad's a giant kettle. Mum
does this thing where she puts a tincy tiny pin in
the bottom of the washing-up bowl and Dad has to
gently move his feet around and relax and watch the
TV, and when he least expects it the pin will burst all
his blisters.

I don't know why you would ever want to pop
your blisters when you least expect it. To pop blisters
is one of the main reasons I am alive. Who doesn't
love bursting those little man-made water balloons
under your feet and letting all the foot juice pour
out? It's incredible. BUT NOT EDIBLE.

Dad says his blisters are really severe and not
like the tiny blisters us lot get. He said these are big
and painful.

Before I head upstairs to put on my pyjamas I call Will again.

Ring.

Ring.

Ring.

And no answer.

Annie adores the phone, so I know they must be out. Maybe their dad took them to Disneyland to say sorry for being so terrible? Or on safari? Let me tell you I will be nothing less than LIVID if Will meets exotic creatures without me. L.I.V.I.D.

But what if their dad convinces them to live with him? Far away? And he never comes back? *Calm down*, I tell myself. *One step at a time.* I run upstairs to snuggle with Lamb-Beth. She is being extra cute and has warmed the bed all cosy for me. But I can tell she is still moody and I bet I know why.

'What do you think of Pork?' I whisper, and give her a gentle nudge. I know this sounds mad but I think she raises an eyebrow at me and shakes her head wearily and sadly. 'Tell me about it!'

Chapter Ten

It is morning now and Pork is the last one to wake up. He is sprawled out on the sofa like a drunken slob. He snores, his tongue lolled to the side of his mouth, his belly rising and falling like a football being pumped up. Hector is amazed by him.

'Doubt there was much mice-catching going on then!' Dad laughs. Dad has a soft spot for the underdog; an underdog means the disadvantaged, the weird ones, the odd ones out. Like me, I guess. Except actually, now that I think about it, I am pretty remarkable.

'I don't know,' Mum says. 'I heard no noises all night, and fingers crossed, haven't seen any new droppings today.'

'Oh, really?' Dad says. 'So maybe Pork's earned the right to a lie-in!'

'Sometimes the mice just sense it, don't they? They can smell a cat a mile away.'

'Can't we all!' I shout, and everybody laughs as the whiffy smell of a milky cat fart wafts over our faces. Lamb-Beth retches a few times and spits. She is not warming to Pork, I can tell.

A thought occurs to me on the way to school. No sign of mice and no sign of Will. It's almost as if the vermin signalled Will's dad's arrival and the vanishing of Will . . . Surely now that the mice have gone, Will should come back too?

And like magic, when I reach the school gates I spot Will's red hair, his slouchy way of standing, his school bag and shoes, and for some unexplainable reason known to man or woman I run. I run really fast, so fast my jaw is juddering and thundering and bouncing and I can't help it, I throw myself around his neck, like two gorillas that have been separated in the wild.

And sneaky leaky pesky tears dribble a bit out of my eyes and I say, 'I'm so happy you're back.' And he pats me politely and tries to make me realize that

we are not on a movie set but in front of everybody at the school gates. He peels me off and I blink a lot and brush myself down and then I say, 'Where have you been?'

Will looks at me blankly and goes, 'Well, erm, I'm here now, aren't I?'

As if nothing had happened. That's how he's acting. As if his dad never turned up at the school gates, as if he hadn't had two days off school and not answered the phone. But worse than that, he isn't being . . . the *same*. It felt like he wasn't my friend any more. Well, that's how it felt. Every time I try to talk to Will about his dad or that morning, he swiftly changes the subject or starts a conversation up with somebody else. I'm trying really hard not to be weird or moody about this, because I have to be patient and remember Will is obviously going through something I can't understand. But it still hurts.

The bell rings furiously for lunch time. Finally, after a morning of fighting for his attention across the room, I can speak to him and we can be normal.

We are the last ones in the classroom; I can feel Will deliberately lagging behind.

'Ready?' I say as he packs his bag away for lunch.

'Ready for what?' he grunts dismissively.

'Lunch. It's burger day!' I smile, but behind the teeth I am frowning.

'I thought I might play football if that's OK?'

My tummy dies. I am flat. Run over. 'Sure,' I croak. In a voice of a person that is NOT OK. 'Sure, that's fine.' And Will nods and still doesn't look up and it's just when I look round at him as I'm walking out of the classroom I see he might be crying but I'm not sure. I wanted to show him my peel taped in the back of my book but the idea now feels too stupid and unwanted.

I am lost. I can't believe I wanted Will to be back at school so much and now that he is, he doesn't even care about me one tiny bit.

To keep my day moving and not be upset I get an extremely vegetarian cheese and pickle sandwich, a packet of Hula Hoops and a juice and go and see Mavis at her desk in Reception. She is happy to see me.

'Where's your Will? Thought you two would be joined at the hip today?'

'Yeah, me too.' I can't hide my disappointment, but I equally don't want Mavis to be nosy. Somehow she isn't and changes the subject.

'I've been so looking forward to this story of yours all night, honestly, it's what got me through my husband's snoring!' I laugh at Mavis; she has this way of looking really serious and then going all soft and smiley again. 'Let's get a brew on, shall we?' A *brew* means tea, but I wish it were a bright purple witch's brew that was served up in a big cauldron!

With a cup of steaming hot tea in one hand, I begin to read Mavis my story. She yawns a little when I start, but I am not offended because that's kind of the intention, I guess, and it proves she's listening as yawning is so infectious. Because Mavis is polite she covers her mouth and lets her eyes do the yawn for

her in little watering puddles. Wow, Mavis has got really leaky eyes. Mavis laughs at the story in these odd places where I didn't even think it was funny and she sometimes closes her eyes. It's also a bit like she's so overexcited that I used a name she suggested for a main character that she almost squeezes her body every time she hears the name 'Morphina', as if giving herself a proud cuddle. I can almost forget

Will ever came back to school and has turned into a completely different person.

'And here's what I worked on yesterday,' I say. 'I've been reading comics, you see, and they inspired me.'

'Comics?' Mavis blurts. 'OK, hen, I can't wait to see what happens. Will the King wake? Will he find out that Morphina is a robber? What will the Queen do? I do like the Queen. She's like me.' Mavis looks proud and does another cuddle of herself.

'OK, I'll continue . . .'

Morphina threw the fine plate of silver that she was holding to the ground with a clatter, her eyes perfectly fixed on the Queen. Their pupils were drawing each other closer, as if there was a light beam connecting their vision.

'How DARE you!' the Queen screeched. 'That belonged to my great-great-grandfather!'

'Get over it,' Morphina teased. 'It's just stuff. This is all nothing but meaningless clutter.'

'You disrespectful toad!' the Queen wailed and let herself fall down the staircase towards Morphina, who was ready and braced her body for the weight of the Queen to charge into her like a rugby tackle.

OOF. The two of them tumbled down onto the stone floor, which was a terribly painful landing. Morphina was winded but she wasn't going to waste a second. She began to beat upon the Queen with her hands, her wrists flailing, her

ring-covered knuckles coming down onto the Queen's head hard. The Queen hoisted her skirt up

high around her legs and used her knees to clamp down Morphina's elbows to the ground like a vice. She was like a fly in a web.

'Ha!' the Queen growled, but before she could begin punching Morphina in the face, Morphina bit her on the forearm so hard it caused blood to drip. The Queen spat as she leaped up like a cat sprayed by a hosepipe, all hairs on end. Morphina then launched herself into the air like a rocket and time seemed to slow as she prepared herself for combat with her tai-chi move *The Death Raven*. Meanwhile, the Queen had begun to undress one of the knights in armour she had on

display, stealing the shield and trying to loosen
the mannequin's grip on the sword.

Morphina hurled her body at the Queen,
whooshing through the air like a wrestler.

'Gosh, it's very . . . erm, *violent*, Darcy.' Mavis
shuddered and pulled her cardigan around her.

'Is it?'

'Yes, very.'

'Good!' I squeaked.

'I think I need another biscuit,' Mavis muttered.
I watched her reach for the biscuits and suddenly
worried that maybe my story was a little gory. Maybe
I'd overstepped the mark a bit with Mavis? Now she
would think I was a disgusting *wee* girl with horrible
thoughts going round in my brain and she maybe
wouldn't give me tea and shortbread any more. I
went to close my writing book.

'What are you doing?' Mavis shrilled. 'Don't
stop!'

I laughed in relief. 'I thought maybe you didn't like it?'

'I may be old but I LOVE a bit of vulgarity! So come on, let's get back to this butt-kicking. I'll tell you what, Darcy, I can think of more than a couple of people I'd like to do this to! Ha-ha! Go on, what happens next?' She nudges me and I carry on reading, with confidence.

The Queen began to cough under the weight of Morphina and her newly acquired shield. The shield smacked Morphina in the head, causing blood to trickle into her eyes. The pair now wrestled like two bears, rolling around on the floor, scratching, punching, kicking, grabbing, pulling, snapping, biting, pinching, prodding, slapping. It was like a hairy snowball of hate that seemed to avalanche around the whole palace; both screaming and shouting abuse.

They rolled towards the open fire. The fireplace was stacked tall with the burning kindle and logs; the ripping roaring flames were orange, gold and yellow, with a flash of electric blue. The Queen forced Morphina close to the fire and her hair began to singe, burning and curling at the ends as a charred black smoke began to billow around them.

'MY HAIR!' Morphina squealed, before drawing a poker out of the fire and smashing it onto the Queen's back a few times, causing the Queen to wail in agony.

'I am THE QUEEN!' she bawled, reaching her hands round Morphina's neck, forcing her further into the fire, like pushing toothpaste onto a toothbrush.

Morphina was actually quite having fun rolling about, but she didn't fancy being strangled or cremated so she forced her hand into the fire to quickly grab a log to set the Queen's frock alight.

The frock lit up immediately and forced the Queen to stand up and begin hopping about as if doing a jig or playing hopscotch. She blew the flames, as if frantically blowing out candles on a birthday cake, but the fire loved the oxygen and it only fanned the flames, causing them to creep up her body.

In blind panic she ran towards Morphina and immediately the flames, like the bond of friendship, latched onto her too; causing them both to go up in tearing heat. The two of them, screaming, ran outside into the palace gardens where the rose garden was in full bloom. The rose heads looked on as the two fire-covered women simultaneously threw themselves into the fountain.

Steam rose off them, like two hot frying pans under a cold tap. Like drenched dogs, their heads like soaking tea towels, their faces exhausted, their dresses charcoaled, crispy and in tatters. Here, in this beautiful elegant setting, with the flowers, the butterflies and hummingbirds and the cloudless sky, the Queen realized there was no maid to clear her up, no gardener to fix the burned lawn that they had turned to ash and nobody to clear the dirtied fountain. Not a soul was awake in the palace to tend to her bruises. Nobody.

The Queen coughed up a mouthful of water and spluttered, 'Well, at least you got him to sleep.' And then she giggled, and so did Morphina – for laughter is as infectious as yawning.

They laughed and they laughed and they laughed, and then they swam in the fountain and laughed some more. Then they ran inside and bathed in bikinis in the giant freestanding hot tub with bubbles up to their chins and didn't once try to drown one another.

Then they tried on loads of the Queen's best fancy party frocks and dressed up in silk

ball gowns. They put on stockings and
pea-coloured high heels, they curled their hair
and did one another's faces, moisturizer,
cleanser, toner, foundation, creamy powder,
bronzer, blusher, highlighter, eye shadow, brow gel,
liner, Kohl crayon, mascara, lipstick and gloss.

Then they ran into the Kitchen, and they
emptied out the larder. They fed on sea salt
and rosemary crackers and chocolate biscuits,
cheese straws, pretzels and jam tarts; they cut
loaves and slathered the slices high with freshly
churned butter and honey. They had grapes and
litres of wine, and turkey and cranberry pie

from the fridge. They gorged on freshly baked still-warm blueberry and orange muffins, lemon mousse, black forest gateaux and pineapple and marmalade ham. They ate nut brittle and sea-salted caramel fudge, coffee and walnut cake and nibbled on the marzipan people that were set to top the fruit cake for tomorrow's afternoon tea.

They had scones and Bakewell tart, pink and white squares of Battenburg cake, and scoop after scoop of raspberry ripple and honeycomb hokey-pokey ice cream. Then they played all of the Queen's favourite songs from her record collection, pretending to 'slow dance' with the great statues of the kings and queens that lined the rooms.

They read each other poetry and did handstands against the palace gates. They filled up party balloons from the store cupboard and blew them up until they were ready to pop. They took the Queen's horses out for a gallop and fed them sugar cubes. They took the lawnmowers out for a spin and raced around the grounds. Then they rode on the same lawnmower and practised some new improvised acrobatics – the Queen tried standing on Morphina's shoulders, for example; it seemed, after their intimate battle, that they were very comfortable with each other's physical strengths.

When night fell they set off fireworks inside 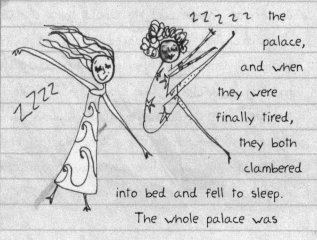 the palace, and when they were finally tired, they both clambered into bed and fell to sleep. The whole palace was asleep now, under the frosted serene dream of peace, the moon winking through the stained-glass windows of every room, sending kite-shapes of colour over every restful face.

When the Queen woke she felt terrible, like she had been hit by a bus. Her bed was covered in paint, glitter, crumbs and even little flecks of blood from her fight with Morphina . . . but there was no Morphina beside her.

What would the King say when he woke up? He would surely send her straight to the doctor, or divorce her! He would think she was a maniac. The Queen looked at herself in the mirror. What a mess. She looked like a child's painting of a clown. She would have to lie to the King; she would have to say it was all a dream, like they do in those long old-fashioned novels. Yes, it was all a big hazy dream. She hopped in the shower and watched the best day of her life swirl down the plughole.

She put on clean clothes and went to face her upside-down palace that she had used like a playground the night before.

'Good morning, your Majesty,' trilled a handmaid.

'Good morning, your Majesty,' said a chambermaid, smiling wide-eyed and sparky.

'Good morning, your Majesty,' said the guards in chirpy chorus.

Everything was spotless, as though nothing had happened at all – what great staff they were, truly top-notch. The butler greeted her warmly and showed her through to the Great Hall. Her husband sat there for breakfast, head of the table, with salmon on a platter before him. Wild Alaskan salmon, her favourite.

'So?' the King smiled.

'I don't know what you're talking about.'

The Queen called for a pot of tea and blew
her nose, as if trying to push the lies out
through her nostrils.

'Did you . . . sleep?' the King asked.

'Did YOU sleep, MORE importantly?' the
Queen snapped back, but the King shook his
head.

'Where's Morphina?' She wanted to know
where her new best friend had got to.

'Who's Morphina?'

The Queen blushed and began to chuckle.
'Don't be silly. Where is she?'

The King shrugged. 'I'm sorry, I don't
know what you're talking about or who this
Morphina is.'

The Queen was confused and cross. The
King just yawned and picked up the newspaper
and there on the front of the paper, the
headline read:

Bounty Hunter and Thief
using guise of Sleep Healer,
using name Morphina,
is prosecuted and Imprisoned
for Great robbery of Palaces

The Queen spat her tea out all over the pink flesh of the salmon. 'There, look, King, look!' she said, pointing, shaking, at the headline.

The King hurriedly put the newspaper down.

'Let me see it!' demanded the Queen. 'See, I told you Morphina was here. I know you don't want to upset me, or perhaps you're embarrassed because you invited her here, but she is my friend and I want to have her released immediately! I command it! Now let me read the article.' The Queen reached for the paper and the King frowned.

'My Queen, I don't know what you think you saw . . .'

'Don't patronize me, let me read it!' the Queen demanded, her voice echoing around the Great Hall as the staff looked afraid and cowered. The King folded the paper away, clearly not wanting the Queen to read it, but she snatched it from him and . . .

THE REAL SLEEPING BEAUTY AT LONG LAST, OUR MAJESTY QUEEN INSOMNIAC SLEEPS A WALLOPING THREE DAYS STRAIGHT, FINALLY OUR KINGDOM CAN RESUME PEACE AT LAST.

The Queen laughed, as if watching a magician do a card trick. 'Oh, silly me. So it was all a dream after all.'

She smiled and helped herself to the salmon, the eye of it blinking at her, the teeth marks on her hand now a scab . . .

'DARCY!' Mavis gasps. 'That's so clever. So it was the Queen all along with the sleeping problems?'

'Yes,' I say.

'I don't know how you do it . . . but Morphina . . . was she real? Because the teeth marks on her hand were from where Morphina bit her, weren't they? Who is she? *What* is she?'

The bell for the end of lunch time shrieks and I pack away my things. I want to show Mavis my copy of *Sleeping Beauty* that gave me the idea for the Morphina story in the first place, but I think this will give me an excuse to go and see her tomorrow lunch time if Will is still not being Will.

'Aren't you going to tell me?' she calls after me, frustrated. I shake my head. In real life, authors don't get to sit next to you breathing down your neck as you read their work, so you don't usually get to ask them questions.

'Ah, you wee tease!' Mavis laughs.

The first thing I am met with when I come out

of the Reception area is the worserest thing I have **EVER** seen that makes me want to scratch my eyeballs out with screwdrivers – Olly Supperidge

and Clementine HOLDING HANDS, and then . . . then . . . THEN . . . SNOGGING. Curse my eyes, my eyes, my sorry scolded red-raw wretched ripped eyesight for chancing upon such a miserable view. Olly Supperidge snogs like a frog, except he is **NEVER** going to turn into a prince like in the fairy tales. He shall remain a wretched bullfrog toad for ever. And anyway the spell wouldn't be broked, as Clementine is NOT a princess queen. She is a ghoul.

They stop the lizard gob-swapping to both take a look at me, all, *Why are you hanging out with MAVIS, AGAIN?* But I think, *SHUT UP, why are you two attaching your lips together? SICK.* They do a bit of whispering and because they are both tall they make me feel like a stumpy turnip. *GO AWAY, you stupid wicked kissing squids!* I start to get angry. ANGRO-SAUR-RUS rex.

And then Clementine tips me over the absolute edge of absolute madness. She's trying to be *caring*, but it's false and patronizing, nosy and mean: 'Great to see Will back at school. Weird, I was expecting you two to be living in each other's pockets . . . but nope . . . not at all . . . it's almost like you two don't even *know* each other. Did you fight?'

'No. We're FINE,' I assure her confidently. And then Olly pulls a face as if to say, *Are you sure about that?*

I walk away.

I am angry with Will and Will's dad, and Annie for not answering the phone or calling me to tell me what was going on. Angry with stupid Olly and wretched Clementine. Angry with the mice and Pork – so angry that I begin to boil up a bit. And Mavis isn't my ONLY friend anyway. Even if Will chooses to never speak to me again I wouldn't care because I've got plenty of mates. I've got LOADS of friends . . . well, there's . . . there's always . . . er . . . I start filing through the faces in my head and realize that at school, apart from Will, my only friend is . . . well . . . Mavis.

Chapter Eleven

'I'VE GOT NO FRIENDS!' are my first words when I enter the house. I stand waiting for Mum to run towards me and burrow me into her armpit and tell me everything will be OK. But she doesn't. 'Mum?'

'In here, Darcy!' Mum calls from the kitchen and she's there, and so, sitting at the table eating a biscuit, is Will. 'What do you call *him*, then?' She smiles.

I want to pretend I'm not happy but I can't. I sort of don't want to ask him why he was weird with me all day because it sort of doesn't matter and 'actions speak louder than words' as my mum always says.

Lamb-Beth is extra happy and licks Will's fingers and rolls over for him to stroke her tummy. There's so much catching up for Will to do – he has to meet Pork and hear about the mice and the kittens at the pet shop! Even though TECHNICALLY he would have heard those stories today if he was my real-life friend and not a weirdo.

Mum puts the Chinese takeaway menu on the table. *Hooray!* I love it that Pork decided for us to have takeaway. I make a list and we all add what we want so that it's all ready and hot for Dad when he gets home. My only-eating-vegetables rule goes out of the window. I am going to EAT, boy! We order so much: chicken balls, crispy duck pancakes, noodles and egg-fried rice. We order stir-fry and chicken in black bean sauce, beef in ginger, and chips too with sweet and sour sauce to dip. We have to get extra of the best sauce that comes with the crispy duck pancakes because it's just too delicious and it's only normal to want to dip absolutely everything into it. Mum gets some other stuff that looks sea-foody

and fishy or too spicy. Whilst we wait for the food to arrive Will and I sit on the stairs by the door like dogs on a door mat waiting for our owner to come home.

'So . . .' I gulp. Feeling a real-life proper actual human conversation beginning.

'Please don't be weird,' he says quietly, stopping me in my tracks. He isn't really wearing gel in his hair. Annie does his hair. Why hasn't he got gel in his hair?

'What? I wasn't!' I defend myself.

'I know that weird voice you do when you're

getting all school counsellor on me.' He blushes, in that purple way he always does.

Even though it's awkward I can't risk not having him open up about this. Detective Darcy tries again . . .

'What did your dad want? I mean . . . why did he come to school?'

'He has kids. More kids . . . new kids . . . with another woman. Two. And he wants us to all be like *friends*.'

'Friends?' I am Will's *friends*. Annie and my family. We're his *friends*. He doesn't need any stupid-not-real borrowed baby brothers and sisters to play happy families with.

'What happened?'

'He wanted us to move with him. To the country-side. Annie and me. To be a family. He said Annie was too young to take care of me.'

'That's not true. Annie's amazing!' I bark. I am a big fan of Will's big sister.

'Well, yeah, I know . . . funny how he didn't care that Annie was *young* when he deserted us. But now it's on his terms he is pretending that he cares.'

'You're not going, are you? To the countryside?'

The letterbox claps. The Chinese takeaway is here and so is Dad. And the conversation is over for now.

There is a five-minute mad rush of excitement as we lay the plates and the cutlery and everything is clattering and banging as we one by one remove the individual cardboard lids and let the hot fragrant steam rise out of each dish.

Lamb-Beth eats prawn crackers, and the sound of her tongue wetting the cracker lets off a little crackling sting, as though there's an electric current running through it. Poppy piles rice into her crackers, scooping it up like the cracker is a forklift truck and the rice is the rubble and her mouth is the dump. Pork nibbles on chicken and then falls back to sleep. I wonder when Henrietta-from-next-door's dog, Kevin, will think to come and harass Pork. Or maybe he will never know he exists as Pork goes outside about . . . ooo . . . OH YEAH, NEVER. The laziest cat in the world.

After Chinese food we are so thirsty we need to drink as many drinks as we can whilst our bodies are set to burst. It feels like I need to open a window in my mouth, let some air in.

'Fortune cookies!' Mum says, and we all settle down on the floor in the living room. We all think

about our future fate that lies inside the cookie. *Hmm* . . . our fingers swirl over them, deciding our destiny. A fortune cookie isn't actually a cookie. It's more like a dried pancake, so crunchy and sweet. Inside they have little slips of paper, messages about your life and stuff.

Hector goes first, but he throws the whole thing into his mouth and nearly chokes, because if it's got sugar in it, he wants it. Dad has to fish it out of his mouth like he's a dog that's stolen a tennis ball; it comes out all slobbery and covered in gob goo.

Dad reads out Hector's fortune whilst Hector eats the cookie. '*Everything has beauty; you just have to find it.*'

'Boring!' Hector ignores it and starts stroking Pork's fur back to front which clearly annoys him as he wakes up to hiss.

Next is Mum: '*Life is a musical and you are on stage.* Am I? Feels like a musical! All this drama. It could be the remake of *CATS*!' We all fall about giggling because of Pork and the kittens at the pet shop, but not too hard in case our stuffed tummies begin to leak food.

Poppy goes next; she opens her fortune and then flushes red. 'I don't want to read this out, this is stupid.' She throws the little slip inside the cookie away, with the cookie too, crunching it up into her hand.

'Don't be silly,' I say. 'Let me see.'

'No, DON'T!' Poppy gargles. 'Please!'

'Oh, just read it.' Mum reaches for her little slip. 'It's only a game.'

'Fine. But it's not true. It says: *Love is in the air for you, ooo-la-la.* See? I told you it was dumb.' And we all laugh, really hard, rolling round on the floor and our bellies hurt even more this time and then Poppy starts to laugh too. 'Dad next!' Poppy instructs.

'OK.' Dad opens his cookie. 'It says: *All your dreams will succeed.* Hope not. I dreamed of being chased by a gorilla last night!' And we all laugh some more.

'Maybe the gorilla is Mum!' Hector yells, and Mum pretends to be offended and grabs him and tickles his belly. He squirms so much his tummy pops out and his bellybutton is all twisted like a knot.

'You go next,' Will says to me.

'No, you go,' I insist.

'Go on . . .' Our fates are being juggled, I think, but I reach for the cookie and carefully unwrap it from the red foil and crack it in two. 'What does it say?' Will asks.

'It says . . . *Keep your future plans a secret* . . . What does that mean?'

'OOOOOOOOOOOOOOO,' Dad says. 'Darcy might run away again with her little witch's hat and twinkly fairy Tinkerbell talcum powder!'

'Shut up, Dad!' I laugh and re-read it again. I can't help but think this cookie was intended for Will, as he is being so secretive about what will happen now his dad has reappeared. I think he is holding something back. 'Now your turn, Will,' I say.

There's only one cookie left, shining like a big fat YES.

'We didn't leave you much choice, did we? Sorry,

Will, our manners are appalling! What are we like?' says Mum, smiling, but Will is used to us and is part of the family anyway.

'*If an awkward moment arises, resort to humour.*' Which makes us all laugh even more, because if there's one thing my family can ace, it is giggling our way out of tricky situations.

We hear a BEEP BEEP HONK outside the house which means it's Annie pulling up to get Will. My heart sinks. I feel sick. And empty. It's like even though Will is here, he isn't *here* here. If that makes sense.

'Aargh, Annie!' Will hops up and goes to put his shoes on and starts thanking my parents and saying goodbye.

'We didn't get to talk properly, I hope everything's OK,' I say as I let him out.

Will looks sad again. 'Everything's fine.'

I nod but I know it isn't. I can't even tell you why it isn't. But I just know. Annie waves at me from the window of her car and I close the door on them.

Poppy is in her bedroom now, with Pork, plan-ning her Friday night sleepover that Pork apparently *demanded*. I go in and flop dramatically onto the bed. I look up at the ceiling. I stare at the light bulb until my eyes go numb, then I close my eyes and can see the white light bulb silhouette on the insides of my eyelids everywhere I look. I do this over and over and over again.

Poppy lies next to me for a bit. 'I'm not cuddling you if that's what you're expecting,' she informs me.

'I wasn't expecting a cuddle.'

'OK, good.'

'Fine.'

'Did you know, Darcy, that because you are now in Big School, you will soon catch spots?'

'Catch spots?' I ask; I never heard of this before.

'Yeah, you'll catch them from all the greasy teenagers. Timothy told me.'

'Oh, right.' I nod. 'Timothy does seem like a person that would know this.'

'But it's OK, I've got your back, you have my full support. I've been inventing, like, in my head obviously, so when the time comes, and you're covered in disgusting grotesque spots, we'll be prepared.'

'How?' I turn to face her.

'You just get the grater, the Parmesan grater, you know, the smaller one for the top of pasta?'

'Yeah?'

'And you just scratch it all over your face.'

228

'What? Really?'

'One hundred per cent.' Poppy looks at her nails as if she's a beauty guru.

'Doesn't it shred your skin?'

'No, because the spots are like ten centimetres tall and so it just shaves them down. It's like filing a nail.'

'Oh, right.' I am satisfied. 'That's a good idea, actually.'

'Thanks.'

In my brain I am thinking, *YOU IDIOT, POPPY! AS IF you would EVER cheese-grate YOUR FACE?! WHAT A STUPID IDEA*. But maybe I'll leave her in ignorant bliss.

I brush my teeth with the wretched spicy tooth-paste and get ready for bed. I keep burping up Chinese food. Gross. Lamb-Beth is snoring on the pillows. I put my fortune-cookie message on my pin board where I keep all my precious things: pictures I like, letters, postcards, ticket stubs. They are spilling out now, all over the walls. Mum keeps telling me off because the wallpaper is getting ruined, but if I see something and I like it, I want to keep it. Sorry about me, Mum. I pull out my writing book and dig out my new old copy of *Sleeping Beauty*. I bet when it was on the shelf in the second-hand bookshop it felt like a Sleeping Beauty itself. Something soooo beautifully sleeping, waiting to be picked up.

I hope that tomorrow everything is good with Will.

Chapter Twelve

The first thing I see when I walk into school the next morning is Will talking to Mavis. I go over.

'There she is. Ah, Will, I tell you, you've got a good friend there. She was so worried about you!' Mavis screeches in her Scottish shrill. 'Poor wee hen.'

Will looks awkwardly at the floor.

'Have you heard her stories? My goodness, Darcy's got an imagination! She's like a living roller-coaster ride!' I am thinking, *How can I unstitch the friendship threads with Mavis now? I'm in too deep. Great.*

Now that Will is back properly I'm sure I won't even ever need to go to Reception so hopefully Mavis will get the message. The bell rings and I'm grateful. We say our goodbyes.

Anyway, Will and I get through maths by using the square gridded paper to design our future homes. We want one big shared complex, but not in a love way, all on one level. Do you ever go to restaurants and imagine what you would do if they were your house? How you would lay it all out? I do. I also have a serious severe addiction: it is also almost physically impossible for me to be in a room and not imagine what it would be like if the ceiling was the floor and the floor was the ceiling. I like to lie on my back and pretend to moonwalk across the roof as if it is the ground.

So Will and I are going to have one big flat house – it might be as long and as wide as a whole floor in our school. I don't like stairs because sometimes when I go up them Poppy will creep behind me and whisper in my ear, 'I'm coming to get you,' and my neck goes all spiky and ticklish and for one quick real sec Poppy isn't my younger sister but in actual fact a monster or a murderer or something. I also would quite like fruit trees all around the perimeter of my house so that I can walk the entire balcony of my one floor and pluck fruit whenever I feel like it. Fresh mangoes, apples, oranges, peaches. Will might want tangerines, I suppose, and then we can frame all the peel spirals he manages to make.

I want a bed that's Goddess size, which is the biggest bed you can get, even bigger than Queen and King and Emperor. It also has sixteen pillows; each pillow has a seam hidden inside with treats sneaked in. Like Maltesers. I want a bubble-bath jacuzzi and a smoke machine. I want a TV that's a circle shape, and it has to be on the ceiling like I'm looking at the moon. I require spontaneous puddles all over the house that are little mini rock pools with crabs and silver and blue fishes darting about inside. I want one room that is a lagoon with crocodiles and a raft that I can paddle about in that has hourly allocated thunderstorms.

Annoyingly, Will wants a football pitch and a

basketball court and a games room. I let him off because one thing I love (not in a married way) about Will is that he's really excellent at making dreams feel a bit realistic. He starts working out the dimensions of our house, using a ruler and then multiplying it by loads to figure out what the real plans are. He thinks we will need several million pounds to make the house happen because there will need to be bedrooms for all my family and one for Annie too. Here are some ways we think we will become millionaires:

1. Go on a TV quiz show where the prize is money.
2. Make fake money out of paper.
3. Hope I might be a writer and have books that people can buy.
4. If the money doesn't work just live on the ceilings of rich people and hope they don't look up.

Quite realistic, I think.

It's lunch time, and Will still hasn't spoken to me about his dad at all and I don't like to ask because I don't want to make him feel weird. When we look at our designs he does that thing again where I think he might cry and this makes me feel so confused. I am finding it hard to navigate this situation: Will is like a maze, a maze that I'm lost in.

'I've got a treat!' His eyes flash and he pulls out two cans of lemonade. Our school has stopped selling fizzy drinks because they say they rot and poison your teeth so it is an absolute real exciting treat to have the cans. It's also more of a treat as today's 'special' on the menu was sludgy gross cold mushroom risotto that sticks to the plates like cement. There is nothing special about that. We don't eat it and the leftovers sit chilling nicely next to us.

Instead we *cheers* our lemonades and knock the top of the can three times each because you have to or else it will explode in your face like a burst water vein. Or is it main?

I wish the lemonade had been chilled before, because it's sticking to my teeth and making them all go furry like mini panda paws. It's harder to drink when it's not cold.

Olly Supperidge slides over. Annoying. But thank goodness he isn't with his new girlfriend . . . come to think of it . . . does Will even know about Clementine and Olly? I pretend Will and I are even more engrossed in our conversation, and then I see poor Koala Nicola on the other side of the room eating a ham sandwich, looking sad and sorry for herself, watching me. I don't want her to think I'm all palled up with Olly these days when I clearly AM NOT. However, I'm also NOT going to whisper any 'advice' into Clementine's ear like what she wants me to do. That's for sure.

'Hi, Burdockington.' Olly curls over me like a giraffe or palm tree: what is this ridiculous nickname he has bestowed upon me? 'When are you going to submit your latest addition to the school magazine?'

'I'll submit when I'm ready,' I say sharply. Will raises his brow protectively. Across the room, Koala Nicola's ears are visibly pricking up like a dog's.

'Cool. I'd like you to come to a meeting. A school magazine meeting. We've had a little, er . . . shall we say . . . team . . . switch-around.'

He coughs in awkwardness. 'And an addition to the team too. I'm really excited about the magazine growing and expanding. Chuffed, to be honest.' He talks like such a vile bank person or politics man off the TV. I can't stand him.

As if on cue Clementine walks into the canteen, and I can tell she doesn't like seeing us talking ONE bit. To be honest, I don't like it either. She screw-faces at me from across the room. Completely raging.

Olly looks round as he sees I've got distracted. He waves a hand to Clementine and says to me, 'So, you gonna put pen to paper or you just going to waste your life bonding with Mavis? Or has she been dumped now that your lover boy's back in town?'

I bite my tongue. He is being extra nasty to show off to Clementine, and knowing that I want to have a lovely day with Will.

Not THIS. I want Will to open up and talk to me and be normal and to just drink my can of lemonade and everything to be good again.

'I'm on it,' I say, to make him leave me alone.

I'm not actually *on* anything. Suddenly I picture myself like a hopeless toad on a lily pad. I see Will confused as to why Clementine is here too. He obviously doesn't know the dreaded news then. That all evils have joined forces in a mission to destroy THE WORLD. Clementine and Olly are boyfriend and (sick) girlfriend. BLEUGH!

Olly stares at our cans of lemonade, disgusted.

'You know rats wee on those, don't you?' he sniffs.

'On what?' Will speaks up this time. His patience has gone.

'The cans. In the factories the rats run wild and wee all over the cans and they don't get washed either, they just get used and used and re-used and used again. They just go round and round recycling rats' wee over and over. So with your lemonade you're also getting mouthful after mouthful of old rancid aged rat wee. Yum yum, tasty.'

'What you trying to say, Olly?' Will shoves his lukewarm can of drink into my hand and stands up quickly.

'No way, this is hys-ter-i-cal.' Olly laughs sarcastically. 'You're not *actually* trying to *size me up*, are you, William Hopper?'

'I asked you a question.' Will is so angry he is as purple as an octopus, the same colour he always flushes when he's panicked or embarrassed or stressed. Just to think Will USED to fancy Clementine. I am forever grateful nothing ever came out of THAT little hiccup.

Other kids in the canteen stop and turn and stare

at the face-off between Will and Olly. Clementine huffs and pouts and then grips Olly's side.

'Will, sit down, leave him, stop it,' I whisper-say.

'They're not worth it, baby,' Clementine hisses, and this makes me really cross and Will surprised. BABY? *BABY?* You are only allowed to say *baby* if you are a member of an American boy band – everybody knows that! Koala Nicola is staring at us with a face that's a mixture of worry with deep pleasure.

Olly can't leave it alone though and goes, 'Makes sense though, doesn't it, William, eh? It's no wonder you're such a misfit – anybody who gets brought up by their sister is bound to be slightly dysfunctional.'

Everybody stands about, blinking. Stunned, in total silence.

Will is so angry; his heart is thudding like a tribe of warriors. He is so mad. He is so Angrosaurus rex. The world is about to pop: Will is like a pot on boil. He is either going to murder Olly or cry. Both will be horrible for him because he will either be in actual or social prison.

Ouch.

But suddenly a ham sandwich comes flying through the air and smacks Olly on the back of the head with a slap. Koala Nicola to the rescue! 'Enough!' Koala Nicola says firmly.

'What?' Olly coughs, his pride knocked out of his head with the weight of a ham sandwich.

'I said, *enough*,' Koala Nicola repeats, stronger this time, and before Olly can answer back Clementine snatches the can of lemonade out of Will's hand and hurls it into Koala's face. Most of it covers her and she screams. Will takes this moment to pick up his risotto leftovers and mush them into Olly's face, and I panic and do the same with mine into Clementine's. Squeezing it right in so that the rice and sludge smooches out of the sides in clumps and the action is up there with my top-ten favourite moments of my life. I don't have time to soak the feeling up because the silly canteen lady in the paper hat has started screaming words like 'detention!', but louder than her words, rumbling over the whole dining hall are these two words which seem far more inviting:

FOOD FIGHT!

I've never had any type of fight before – well, maybe when I threw a rubber at Jamie Haddock, but that was in baby school so it doesn't count. And not a fight with weapons . . . if you can call food a weapon, which I'd say this manky risotto definitely was. But when I look around to see Will and Clementine, goody-goody Koala Nicola and pretty much everybody else in the room chucking yoghurt and muffins and sliced tomato, I can't just stand by and watch now, can I? I reach for a neglected bowl of noodles next to me, launching them into the air like a grenade of slimy worms.

A scoop of mashed potato smushes Will right in the eye and I am hiding behind the table, popping up to lob various food items like lighting grenades; an apple core spinning through the air, whacking some boy I always see but don't know the name of in the shoulder – MAN DOWN.

A ball of tinfoil skids across the table and taps Chloe from my class on the ankle – *Sorry, Chloe.* She is a weakling though, so nothing to worry about there, revenge-wise. Risotto hits a few more faces, half a chocolate bar boofs Tony Lyson in the cheek and I duck so he can't see it was me that made it land there. A handful of salad springs into the air like a firework exploding and a handful of chips confetti the sky, raining down onto some older kids.

A spinning dry triangle of pizza . . . oooo . . . this

is good . . . frisbees into Olly's face right on the jawbone. Will winks at me. If I could choose a moment to live in for the rest of my days it would be that moment and certainly not the next moment where a jacket potato flies through the chaos and hits me right in the face

and my nose begins to bleed. With, yes, BLOOD. AHHHHHHHHHHHHHHHHHHHHHHHHHH-HHHHHHHHHHHHH! The worst jacket potato filling. Ever.

An ear-piercingly high-pitched whistle is blown. Will drops the can he is holding and it clatters to the floor in slow motion, spilling its guts into the cheap custard and baked-bean stained carpet.

I gawp, the sound stops and everything hurts, and I just see Will turn to me and his eyes lower like he's ashamed and full of regret and worry. Blood rivers into my mouth from the wound caused by the dangerous jacket potato. I try not to cry. I can taste metal.

Olly walks away because he can sense the shock, swearing because he doesn't care any more and it's too late to be worried about getting in trouble. Clementine, who looks like she could have another round, is pacing, foot to foot, fist in mouth, hungry for more. Koala Nicola is crying. Dribbling again. And the rest of the hall are checking their ketchup-stained injuries, bleeding mayonnaise and tartar sauce, oozing gravy.

The dinner lady in the paper hat stands on a chair to give her monologue of anger. She tells us that she is DISGUSTED and HORRIFIED and NEVER IN HER LIFE OF ALL THE 17,890,462 SCHOOLS THAT SHE HAS

WORKED IN HAS SHE EVER and I repeat
EVER, SEEN SUCH DEPLORABLE AND
DESPICABLE BEHAVIOUR!

She demands to know who started it, and Clementine has no trouble telling the whole story: all about us fighting and, of course, her favourite part, 'Then Nicola threw the ham sandwich at Olly's head and that's when things got nasty.'

And Koala Nicola is sobbing more and more and starts telling the lady in the paper hat the whole entire love story like she's on a chat show, and as though the woman in the paper hat *cares* that Clementine *stole* Olly from her.

Apparently, the five of us (the infernal love triangle plus Will and I) are the 'instigators' and have a 'serious punishment' ahead of us, and blood is still pouring out my nose and my eyes are watering. The dinner lady says, 'First things first,' and points to me. 'Get this girl to the school nurse!' But when Will tries to take me she says, 'NOT YOU! YOU ARE IN DEEP DEEP TROUBLE, I'M AFRAID.' And that's when

Will drops a bombshell on me that hurts more than any jacket potato.

'I don't care anyway; today is my last day at this school. I'm leaving. Leaving to live with my dad in the country, so give me whatever stupid punishment you want to because it WON'T MAKE A DIFFERENCE.'

Will's words fall to the ground like autumn leaves. Slowly. Leaving emptiness behind them.

Will grips me tighter, cradles me close – it's the closest we've ever been BUT still not in a love way . . . I feel sick and ill and terrible and realize Will is the only thing holding me up. I'm not sure if it's my battle wounds or my heart that is hurting more. Will says something right into my ear but I can't hear it. I don't hear it. I don't hear anything. I don't hear anything at all.

Chapter Thirteen

Dear Diary,

   Today is my birthday. I am ninety-nine.
How time does fly. I woke up lovely and
early at 5 a.m. because as soon as you get
past the ripe age of fifty-five it is practically
illegal to have a lie-in. Mavis, my best friend,
is 154 now and so it's not so easy for us to
celebrate a birthday how we used to. She still
bakes plenty of shortbread and we have lots
of tea but we don't dance any more or wear
high shoes.

For breakfast we had grey porridge but with prunes on top as a treat. Prunes in addition to being sweet also help to 'keep things moving', if you get my drift, and so there were lots of good old steamy nanny farts chiming their way out of us all morning. I did suggest sprinkling some hazelnuts on top too, but even the sight of the nuts can bring tears to Mavis's eyes — her teeth just couldn't manage them, and she's barely managed to break the husk of a walnut since Christmas.

By 7 a.m. we were sitting by the log fire with the cats and the newspapers. Mavis can't read very well any more as her eyes are tired and so I read the words out as loud as I can, but Mavis can't hear very well so I have to repeat the words over and over. Sometimes I've repeated the words so many times that by the end of the sentence that I've repeated she has forgotten completely what the sentence is about and so that's a waste

of time and a very frustrating way to spend a
birthday that can often end in migraine.

Later, we play some records and Mavis and
I have tea and sing to the music. Sometimes,
if we turn the music up too loud, one of us
can get quite overexcited and our dentures fall
out. This happened to Mavis today, but I
tried to see the positives and managed to make
a bit of a party game out of it: chasing the
dentures around the floor was quite similar
to Pin the Tail on the Donkey. Next, when we
had calmed down, we had a nap and I did
that thing I do most days when I wake from
my nap, which is to immediately assume that
Mavis has died in her sleep but, alas, she
had not.

We have more tea and then Mavis
remembered she had got me a present, but
her memory is not very good so she couldn't
exactly recall where she had hidden the gift,
which was a little disappointing. It seemed

a lovely sunny day and we decided to have a lovely picnic lunch in the garden. I've always loved nature. When Mavis and I first met, at school, I was a pupil and she was the receptionist – we're talking a good eighty, eighty-five years ago now – and we used to love cheese and pickle sandwiches. We always eat them on birthdays and celebrations. Now, in our older years, the bread has to soak overnight in milk to soften, otherwise it's far too tough to chew and even the freshest bread can feel like eating a house brick for us. The cheese also has to be gently warmed in the oven too. Once the sandwiches were prepared we tried to get outside, but both of us kept taking turns to fall over. This was reasonably stressful. I certainly saw Mavis's knickers more times than I wanted, however we were past embarrassment in our old age.

By the time we eventually managed to make

it into the great outdoors, the sun had gone in and so we had to turn round and come back in again. We ate our milky sandwiches propped up against the washing machine because it was too exhausting to get to our chairs. Next, Mavis thought that it might be fun to do some girly spa treats for each other. Mavis said she would give me a manicure, and although I was rarely one for spas, I always enjoyed painting my nails. The manicure was pretty pathetic and didn't really make much of an impact, as Mavis's wrists are so weak these days she can barely hold a file. I suggested we moved to the nail paint and that too wasn't a great success as Mavis couldn't open the lid of any of the varnishes. After a good old tug and with the helpful grip of a tea towel we managed to open up the multi-coloured varnishes and Mavis tried to paint my fingernails. However, she was shaking so much that she painted my whole fingers and

hands and the carpet and armchair and cat and rug.

'Thank you, Mavis.' I smiled to be polite as I could see that the manicure had really taken it out of her and I suggested we swap so that I could paint her nails. The moment I touched the nail file on her fingernail the nail came off in one crumbling puff. It didn't hurt Mavis as she didn't even realize it had happened. There was no blood, just dust.

I suggested we watched a girlie movie to cheer us up. I would have preferred something more dramatic like *Jurassic Park* but Mavis has a very jumpy heart and so we had to watch quite slow-paced romantic comedies, but nothing too romantic or comedic that would get her too frazzled. Within the first minute Mavis was snoring and I drank more tea and stroked the cat and pretended to admire my painted 'manicured' hands.

I thought about eating a celebratory toffee but couldn't be bothered with the stress of having to get the toffee out of my teeth. Then I decided I was bored and could do with the challenge and so I ate one anyway. When Mavis woke she remembered where my present was and we both got excited and tried to make it up the stairs together where Mavis said the present would be 'waiting' at the top of her wardrobe. This confused me, as Mavis hadn't been upstairs for several years. She seemed really determined to find the present and she had set my pulse racing too with suspense, and so we climbed the Everest of steps.

Sweating and tumbling, groaning and moaning, our bodies creaking like old rusty scissors, we finally reached the top and then Mavis forgot why we had come up the stairs and I reminded her, 'We're looking for my birthday present. It's my birthday.'

And Mavis suddenly yelled, 'Why didn't you say so? Happy Birthday!' And she was elated and over the moon and it was then that it dawned on me that it was impossible for Mavis to have got me any kind of present as we hadn't left each other's side for twenty years. Still, there wasn't anything else to do, and we had come this far.

Mavis and I crept into her bedroom and it was like we were robbers breaking into a museum. Everything was in its place. Cobwebbed and forgotten like a ship at the bottom of the

sea. Her dressing table, the mirror, the jewellery
and make-up. Mavis touched her belongings and
I redirected her to the wardrobe. Mavis opened
the wardrobe and we were really tired now.
We had indulged in an exhausting day full of
activities and fun and it was beginning to take
its toll. Mavis began to rummage through the
wardrobe full of her old dresses and shoes and
handbags. The smell of mothballs and dust and
memories floated out of the wardrobe like spirits.

Then Mavis, with her watery eyes, her
papery skin and her powdered cheeks, looked
to me and said, 'Ah, I remember now, your
present is certainly up here – it's *there*.'
Mavis pointed to the window and I travelled
my eyes from her finger to the sky, and through
the net curtains was a rainbow. It was a
beautiful present and I couldn't have asked
for anything more.

I looked my best and only friend Mavis
right in the eye, saw years of understanding

and history. I could tell that she was tired. 'Shall we sleep up here?' I suggested, pointing to her bed.

'We couldn't do *that*.' Mavis looked taken aback. 'We sleep downstairs in our chairs, remember, you wally!' She chuckled.

'Yes, I know, but you're tired and it's my birthday and I thought it would be nice to sleep flat out, in a bed.'

'Is that what you want?' Mavis asked.

'Yes, I think so.'

We both crept into the bed like two mad old dogs. It took far less time than I had

> anticipated because we were exhausted.
> We lay down, back to back like two crinkled
> crumpled prawns. Sleep began to wash over
> us and just before we nearly fell to sleep
> Mavis said, 'Darcy, you'll be one hundred
> next year.'

I throw my writing book down. It's been Friday all day and I've not been to school because we were all suspended and are not allowed to go back until Monday.

Except Will. He goes back to school NEVER.

It feels like a sick day or a no-day. Just an empty weird pillow day. I am devastated. Ill. Sick. *What will I do without Will?* He is my kind, my species, my same, and now he is going, going, gone. Without even a warning, a proper goodbye, a send-off. I can't even properly speak to anybody about it because

I'm just a *naughty suspended girl who had a food fight,* and what's worse is that Mum and Dad won't even shout at me or tell me off properly. I mean, who is going to shout at their daughter who got injured by a vegetable? Pathetic.

I had wanted to call Will all day but Mum and Dad were strict about that one. I kept seeing myself waving goodbye to Will as Annie's car threw itself down the street, and I was puffed out like a cloud from the exhaust pipe. Distant and left behind. That was it.

All day I've been feeling so sorry for myself and upset. Slumping and flumping around the house in my home clothes. I look like a man with a stubbly unshaved chin, who gets fired from his job and divorced, like the ones on TV who walk around in their pants and dressing gowns drinking milk from the carton without even taking the time to look for a glass. Even when they find a glass they are all dirty. Or smashed. That's me.

Looking in the fridge only to find nothing for me to eat because everything is reserved 'for Poppy's mates', because it's the night of her sleep-over – yes, the one that PORK THE CAT ARRANGED.

I feel sooo drained and slobby, like Pork who is lazing on the armchair. We have an awkward moment of eye contact. We both don't blink. This will be my first-ever staring competition with an animal; then again there is a first time for everything. Mum suggested rainchecking the sleepover but Dad said he would rather 'get the stupid thing out the way'. Besides, it's always raining.

It's later on and I'm back up in my prison cell of a bedroom. I'm livid now instead of sad. I am cross at Will for not warning me he was leaving and for telling me at the same time as everybody else. I'm not even technically allowed to enjoy the sleepover either because realistically I am in punishment period until Monday. All I can hear is *giggle giggle giggle. Ha-ha-ha-ha-ha. OOOOOOO.*

Why does Poppy have to be so popular? One of her stupid friends is allergic to cats too – she can be in the same house as a cat, but can't touch one apparently – well, suits me as I am officially allergic to happiness. I can be in the same house as it, I just can't touch it. Apparently. Anyway. So I have to be stuck with Pork in my bedroom to make sure he doesn't escape because Poppy and her mates have taken over THE WHOLE ENTIRE HOUSE. Lamb-Beth is clearly fuming. I can't stop looking at the future house plans that Will and I made for our house in the back of my maths book. Tears blubber in my eyes. Big fat inconvenient ones. I want to scribble all over the plans and just throw them in the bin but I know that I'll really regret that. So I quickly get a pen and write in massive letters next to the plans:

YOU WALK
I WALK
YOU RUN
I RUN
YOU EAT
I EAT
WE ARE ONE HUMAN
    BEAN, YEAH
I SEE
YOU SEE
I LIE DOWN
YOU LIE DOWN
I DRINK
YOU DRINK
I THINK
YOU THINK
YOU GO
I GO
I AM HERE
YOU ARE HERE
WE ARE TOGETHER.

Wqqqaaa

And then I just let myself cry. I cry and cry and cry and cry. My body releases like a huge humungous tap. I outdo Koala Nicola a million times over as I let my face become a waterfall and I just sob. Hard. I find a rhythm in the crying, a rocking, heavy, breathy one. *Ouch ouch ouch. My heart. My heart.*

Lamb-Beth is lying with her back to Pork, trying to soothe me and comfort me and Pork is doing that annoying thing that cats do when they try to get comfy and press their paws into every single space a matrillion times, like they are rolling out pizza dough. Has he no social awareness? Can't he see I'm a mess?

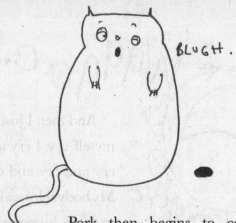

BLUGH.

Pork then begins to cough/choke, retching and spluttering. Lamb-Beth throws him daggers and pokes out her tongue as he sicks up a huge hairball. It globber slobbers onto my carpet. GROSS. Lamb-Beth rolls her eyes and burrows deeply into her body. Pork has tipped her over the edge. Me too. That monstrous horrible creation has annoyed me enough this week! I've had enough. Everything has gone wrong since stupid Pork entered our life. *Everything!*

'Pork, this is why you shouldn't lick your own skin all day, you stupid doormat tongue, because look at you!' I shout through the tears. Pork ignores me and stretches onto his back and farts some more.

'You don't even care, do you?' I shout at Pork, and I am absolutely right – Pork just Does. Not. Care. 'I am sick of you, Pork!' I continue. 'You are NOT a good friend to Lamb-Beth, just like how Will is NOT a good friend to me and because of that you can go!'

I want to boot him out of my bedroom, but that stupid weakling friend of Poppy's with the cat allergy means I can't. Just looking at the furball sick on the floor is making me madder and madderer. So I pick Pork up and I carry him downstairs and into the kitchen, and I don't think once or twice or at all as I just throw him into the garden. 'Be sick out THERE!' I mutter under my breath. He is a cat not a prince. For some reason he hadn't been let outside yet because he needed to *acclimatize*, but he is an animal, so he needs fresh air like Lamb-Beth. I'll let him back inside in half an hour anyway, once I've calmed down.

I get a sponge off the sink and some cleaning spray that Mum uses to clean the sides and march back upstairs. Mum catches me as I am going up. She pops her head out of the living room where all of Poppy's *fun* is taking place.

'You going to come down?' she asks.

'I'm not allowed, am I? I'm grounded,' I snub.

Mum can see I've been crying. To be honest, you'd have to not know what crying was to think I hadn't been.

'You're still technically on the *premises*,' she reminds me, smiling. She's trying to cheer me up. Obviously she doesn't know that I am immune to joy.

'You're not a police officer, so stop it,' I say back smartly.

'Watch your attitude, please.' Mum gets firm.

I drop my head to the floor. 'Sorry.'

Mum looks at me and softens. 'Come down?

Poppy's friends are dying to meet you. Timothy has bigged you up like you're an A-List celeb!'

'Yeah, maybe. Once I've cleaned up Pork's annoying vomit.'

Mum bites her lip, trying not to laugh, and I elephant-step myself up the stairs.

After cleaning the sick I come back downstairs to talk to Mum and see what leftover snacks I can scavenge from Poppy's sleepover. *Why is she having a sleepover anyway? What? Because Pork demanded one?* If Pork told her to jump off a bridge, would she do it? Pork isn't even allowed to go to his own sleepover anyway. Ridiculous.

I let my eyes flit to Hector; he is always doing something weird to cheer me up. Today he is a bit 'under the weather' so he gets Calpol. I am livid with jealousy as Calpol is liquid sweeties that make you better and you're only actually allowed it when you are ill. I am not allowed that any more, either. When I'm sick now I have to drink this wretched cough mixture that tastes like lizard and buffalo blood.

'Can I have some?' I ask Mum, and point at the Calpol.

'No. You're not sick,' Mum says.

'I feel like I am.' I bang my head on the table, sad mixed with anger mixed in with frustration.

'Let's talk,' Mum says, and fills the teapot, which is her symbol of settling down for *talking*.

'I don't want to,' I grumble.

'OK.' Mum puts the silly tea cosy on top of the pot to keep the pot all warm. It's really old-fashioned but so cute I just can't take it. 'I saved some biscuits for you before the Gremlins got to them.' She pulls out a plate of cookies and the shrill of Poppy and her mates seems to get a pitch louder.

'Well, I GUESS I could talk,' I start. 'I don't think I have any friends and Will's left now . . . I didn't even get to say goodbye properly and why didn't he warn me sooner . . . and now that he's gone . . . I don't want to have to be best friends with Mavis the receptionist.'

Mum laughs. 'Don't be silly. Firstly, you have lots

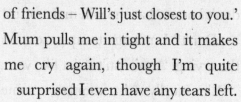

of friends – Will's just closest to you.' Mum pulls me in tight and it makes me cry again, though I'm quite surprised I even have any tears left. 'Not any more. He might start doing that weird thing again where he pretends he doesn't know me.' I pick at the dried blood around my nostril, it's quite calming.

'Don't do that, that's vile.' Mum taps my wrist.

'It's blocking my breathing passage,' I say. It isn't really. I stare at the little pile of enjoyable noseblood crust. 'He could have called me all day or popped round but he hasn't!'

'He's not allowed, your school said so, that Scottish lady at Reception called us all and gave us strict instructions.'

'THAT'S MAVIS!' I yell.

'Oh, she's your new best friend, is she? Wow, I

don't know what she will make of us!'

'Don't!' I manage to squeeze a smile out through the crying. 'Annie isn't strict like you and Dad.'

'I'm hardly strict, monkey – some parents would have been *really* cross. Dad and I let you off because we knew you were hurt and the house has been hectic with . . . everything.'

'Pork.' I help her out.

'Yeah, Pork.'

'What I mean is, Will would have called. If he wanted to speak to me, he would have found a way, or got on his bike and come.' I pick at a biscuit with the same hand I used to scratch the blood, remember before it meets my mouth and stop. Mum breathes out loud in a deep sigh because she knows that's what Will would have done. I a bit cry.

'He pushes you away because he wants to make it easier for you both, like tearing off a plaster, quick and effective. He is trying to *wean* you off him so it isn't as hard.'

'Like a werewolf,' Hector butts in.

'No, *not* like a werewolf – this has nothing what to do, whatsoever, with werewolves,' I snuffle. 'What are you drunk on? Calpol?'

'He has a point actually, Darcy.' Mum considers. 'You see how werewolves are human in the day, then in the night, when the moon comes out, they turn into wolves?'

'Yes . . . ?' My family make no sense.

'Well, you know how often they might be with a friend or meet somebody nice, somebody they don't want to hurt and before they turn into a wolf, once they see the moon, they tell that person to RUN, to run before it's too late and they get gobbled up?'

'Yes . . . ?' Oh no. Where is this going?

'And the person never understands because they aren't to know that they are in the company of a secret werewolf. They get upset and confused, and they don't see that the wolf is telling them to run away as fast as they can, to save themselves from getting hurt. Well, that's what Will is doing with you. Will's trying to push you away so you won't get hurt.'

'Will is a werewolf?'

'No!' Mum laughs and pours the tea.

'Yes.' Hector nods. 'I always knew he was cool.'

'You should write a story for Will, Darcy – something for him to take with him. Turn the negatives into a positive. Write something about him being a strong wolf! A strong wolf that protects you no matter what!'

And that doesn't seem like such a bad idea.

As a baby he was like no other. He howled instead of crying, growled instead of moaning and purred instead of laughing. He was a savage. He broke all of his toys and rolled in the mud and liked to sleep on the floor instead of in his bed.

When he got a little older he couldn't go to nursery because he bit the faces and hands and feet of his classmates, but that wasn't because he wanted to hurt them, it was how

he played. Just like a
wolf. But the trouble
was, the other boys
and girls in his

AAAA!

Wooops.

classes weren't wolves and they didn't want
to be bitten, thank you very much, and so they
had to take him out of nursery and his mum
would spend the day with her beloved son.

He liked to walk around on all fours, like
a dog or cat. When he went to the park he
would run into the pond and start roaring
at the ducks and geese, causing a flap, and
he would leap and pounce in the grass for
hours on end, launching into the air and then
prowling about. For his dinner he always asked

for meat and milk –
he would eat the
meat raw with
his hands and
wouldn't even leave
behind the tangly strings of
fat. He would lap the milk up from a bowl
on the floor and any mess he made he would
clear up with his tongue.

It became pretty clear that this boy was
like no other – this boy was like a wolf, and
so they nicknamed him *Wolf*.

Sometimes, so they could dine at nice
restaurants and do normal tasks like going
to the supermarket, Wolf's mum and dad
tried to make him calmer, more polite and
well-mannered.

Wolf refused to be what he wasn't, because
it wasn't who he was. And his parents grew
to understand their son's ways and they soon

didn't want Wolf to be any different either, so they learned that they had to let their son be free to explore, to wander and roam.

As he was growing older and no longer went to school, Wolf's dad built him a huge jungle gym in the garden. A giant wooden construction with slides and swinging tyres and long grass, and Wolf would spend all day learning to hunt and burrow and delve.

After some time Wolf began to understand that he was different and that maybe it was a bad thing. And people began to stay away from this weird boy that didn't go to school and spent all day in the garden and ate raw meat. Wolf's parents were devastated because their son was being shunned. They couldn't explain. They felt responsible. Nobody wanted to give their son a chance.

One night Wolf picked at his raw bloody steak but he didn't have much of an appetite.

He had lost the flush from his cheeks and the
sparkle in his eye. Dinner was eaten in silence,
with just the painful sound of the clock ticking
away the slowing seconds. It was an early
night for Wolf's parents. Did you know
nothing is more exhausting than worry of the
head? You could run up a mountain and
you would still never even get close to the
exhaustion of an over-worrying or saddened
head. Wolf didn't sleep. He stared at the
moon and longed to howl to it, in hope that
the moon might sing back once, to answer all
of his misery.

'I want to go back to school,' he said
over his breakfast of liver. He hadn't spoken in
months, so he must have been serious.

'But, Wolf, we discussed that. School
and you is like a can of petrol and a flame.
They don't mix. It always ends badly.'

'I am ready. Please give me a second
chance,' he pleaded, and his eyes meant it. He

did look so unhappy and deflated – he hadn't smiled in ages.

His parents looked at each other in deep fear and apprehension. *What was the right decision?* He was nearly a teenager now and had missed so much of school. Would he even know how to be around his own kind?

Wolf set foot onto the school grounds to the soundtracks of giggles and gossip. To the whispers and murmurs, the taunts and sniggers. He hung his head low. This was harder than he had thought . . . *Had he made a mistake? Had he freaked everybody out so much that there was no going back? Was this a bad idea?*

And all day long he felt like he was being followed by snipers – evil judging menacing faces seemed to watch his every move. He was under the microscope and he felt like a bug being poked at with a set of tweezers. This was a harsh experiment and he was the subject.

This wasn't going to work. He realized that when he went to the canteen at lunch and nobody wanted to sit next to him. Even he knew that they knew that his choice of cheese omelette wasn't going to hit the spot. He felt himself begin to cry but he sucked the tears back. They didn't deserve a single drop.

It was nearly winter and was already dark outside even in the late afternoon, and for Wolf, coming home from school was even worse. At least at school, under the supervision of teachers and authority, it meant his day had some kind of monitoring, no matter how weak it was. But after school, the walk through the park was a complete free-for-all and the bullying continued. Names were called; sticks and sweet wrappers were thrown at his back. This was such a bad idea. His life was over. Surely.

Then he heard a whimpering, a small noise, a sobbing. *What was this?* Probably some evil trick to lure him in by the bullies. He tilted his head to see behind the bushes, and by the train tracks were three boys, big ones, older than him, with two smaller boys up against trees. He watched on as the big boys called the little ones 'weak' and 'idiots'. They wanted the little boys' money and phones and house keys. The little boys were crying and were scared.

Wolf gulped. He believed he could take these boys on, but what if it went wrong and the little ones got frightened of him? What if he was pinned up against a tree himself, begging for his life? He was supposed to be invisible, playing it down, keeping a low profile.

'I'll kill you. Do you understand?' one of the big boys said to a shaking little one. 'I swear, I will kill you because I don't like gingers and I don't like weaklings.'

The little boy cried more and nodded and let

tears shower down his cheeks. This made Wolf FURIOUS. He felt a burning rage in his belly and he grunted.

The little boy caught his eye and he lost his breath. *It was the WOLF boy that everybody had been speaking about at school, he was here. He was going to eat him up! The rumours were true!*

The other little boy saw Wolf too now, and his teeth began to chitter-chatter in terror and tears jingle-jangled in his eyes. The boys gripped their necks tighter, enjoying the fear that was sweeping across the boys' faces as it meant they were making an impact, gaining power. One of the little boys had a cut on his head from one of the bullies and blood began to trickle.

This made Wolf even madder and he had to get the attention of the boys. He put a finger to his lips: 'Shhhhhh,' he reassured.

But it was too late. The bullies had seen Wolf's reflection in the little boys' eyes and they couldn't believe their luck. They weren't scared of this freak, and instantly the little boys were dropped, clattering to the ground like empty fried-chicken boxes.

'You're just in time,' one of the bullies said. 'We were planning on cooking up a feast.'

'Yeah,' the other scoffed. 'In your honour!'

'Two little idiots.' The biggest bully laughed and kicked at the trainer of one of the little boys.

'Now there's no point because we heard you like to eat your meat raw anyway.'

They all laughed. Wolf pushed past the big boys and went to grab the little ones, to rescue them.

'I don't think so, FREAK.' The bullies
scooped Wolf up by his shoulders and pinned
him to the ground.

'Get off me!' Wolf yelled. Suddenly he felt
very weak, light and harmless. All his strength
seemed to evaporate out of him. He felt like
a floppy rag doll with shoelaces for arms
and legs.

'Do you know what it will do for our
reputation to take down the wolf boy? We will
be the most powerful kids in school,' one of the
big boys grunted.

'Come on, is this all you've got?' Another

prodded him in the chest. 'Aren't you meant to be all strong and that?'

The boy was right. *Where had his strength gone?* Especially when he needed it the most. He was being ruined by three big bullies. He had let the other boys down. School tomorrow would be even worse once people found out that he was feeble. Wolf shouted to the little boys, 'RUN! RUN AS FAST AS YOU CAN! RUN HOME! RUN HOME NOW! DON'T LOOK BACK, JUST RUN! RUN! RUN!' and the little boys suddenly, as if miniature balloons had burst over their faces, unlocked themselves out of the hypnotism of fright and began gathering themselves up, and just as they were about to start running the weirdest most unexpected thing happened.

Through the bushes lit the yellow electric eyes of a big group of wolves. Their snarl, their growl, their teeth glistened. They stepped forward, their ears pricked, their noses sniffing.

 Wolf's jaw dropped and he felt his body loosen – he had never seen a real wolf before.

The bully boys naturally loosened their grips and began to fall to the floor.

'W-w-w-w-wolves . . . but . . . ?'

The wolves stepped closer. They could smell fear, and it stank and filled their noses up. It was an insulting and repulsive stench. They came closer, sniffing the bullies out. And then, through the shadows, the leaves, brambles and oaks, more and more wolves came.

The bullies closed their eyes. They had frozen in time, their bodies cold wet dead fish, their hearts in their mouths. One of the wolves then looked to Wolf and bowed his head.

It was a respectful nod and suggested to Wolf that he should take the small boys home. Wolf did as he was told. One of the bullies gulped frantically and tried to escape too, but a wolf had a heavy paw on his jacket. And he wasn't going anywhere. Wolf regained his strength, and with a boy in each arm ran, ran through the park and back to his home, with the howls of the wolves rattling through the leaves.

Wolf, at school now, was a hero. Everybody wanted to be his friend because he was special and unique. He wasn't excellent at maths or particularly good at art, but he was amazing at PE and play time, funny to watch at lunch time, and took a starring role in the school's production of *Little Red Riding Hood*.

P.S. The bully boys were not eaten. They were just warned, which in life is a far better lesson.

I close my writing book. I like to think of Will as a wolf, sending wolves to protect me from far away, wherever I might be. Feeling a little better for now, I peep my head round the door of the living room where Poppy's sleepover is in full swing. I should say hello to my audience. I feel like I am skulking around my house at the moment. A grounded punished rebel feral child who got a detention and a bleeding nose, like one of those problem kids off TV, although they probably don't get their war wounds and battle scars from flailing baked potatoes.

'Hi,' I say.

It is mayhem. Poppy and Timothy are dressed in matching leotards and are standing on the sofa

holding candlesticks as microphones. All of Poppy's mates are in sunglasses, clapping and dancing. There are clothes and sweets and biscuits and dolls and teddy bears and toys and books and wigs and feather boas and stuff EVERYWHERE.

'DARCY! You're HERE!' Timothy squeals. 'Come and play, we're having a talent competition, and you can be the judge!'

'I don't think so . . .' I say politely.

'Come on, it will be fun!' Timothy pleads. 'But first clean the scabs off your nose, babe – this isn't a midlife-crisis TV show!' It is impossible to be cross with Timothy. 'Come on, honey!' he shouts, and then all of Poppy's friends start chanting, 'DARCY! DARCY! DARCY! DARCY!' and you know what . . . for a second I consider it. Then Lamb-Beth skids into the living room and starts nudging at my leg. A lot.

'What is it?' I say to her, as if I can understand. Lamb-Beth begins tugging at my sleeve with her teeth.

'Turn the music off, Timothy!' Poppy orders. 'Everybody be quiet.' Lamb-Beth *never* does anything like this.

'What's wrong?' I ask, and then Lamb-Beth does the weirdest thing. She bleats. She bleats, '*Merrrr. Merrrrr. Meerrrrrrrrrrrrrrrr.*' Over and over and over again. '*MERRRRRR. MERRRRRRR. MEERRRRR.*'

'She's bleating!' Timothy says. 'She's trying to tell us something!'

Lamb-Beth pulls at my sleeve again, wanting me to follow her. 'Come on, then . . .' I let her lead the way. We walk into the kitchen and Mum frowns as she sees the trail of us, all of us, including Poppy's mates, dressed up.

'What's all this?' she asks, hugging her mug close.

'Lamb-Beth is trying to show us something outside.'

And then we hear the howling from outside and

we open up the back door and Henrietta-from-next-door throws her head over the fence and says, out of breath, 'I'm so sorry! Kevin . . . it's Kevin. My dog. He attacked your cat.'

Chapter Fourteen

You couldn't make the scene up. Pork is sprawled
out on the sofa dressed in Hector's pyjamas, looking TOO comfortable and feeling TOO sorry
for himself, being pampered by all six of Poppy's

friends and
having the
time of his
absolute life.
If there was a cat
heaven, it was
here right now.
Being stroked and
petted and fed

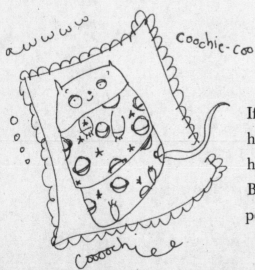

awwww

coochie-coo

coochie

milk, and sheet after sheet of ham, and fork after fork of tinned tuna. Yes, Pork did have the odd scratch and his tail was a little bent out of place, but other than that we could find nothing more than a broken whisker. To be honest he looked better than ever – the fright seemed to give some kind of flush to his cheeks, which made him look more sparky than his usual drowsy state.

Lamb-Beth was the most frazzled as she lay shaking from the shock next to Pork, getting an equal amount of cuddles and attention, but mostly a bit *put out* that she had shown some emotion towards the furry dumpling that is Pork. Their relationship started to remind me of my own relationship with Hector and Poppy, how you can row with them and be mean and nasty but you still don't want them to get hurt. You still care. Pork's purr was so loud it was like a car alarm that nobody could switch off.

Poppy's friends were over the moon to be invited to our 'mad house' where cats wear pyjamas.

'We should charge an entrance fee for the next

sleepover, Darcy; you get the full works here! The entertainment is five stars, it truly is an all-round experience!' Timothy cackles. 'This is such a wild house, you guys are the hostesses with mostesses!'

This makes Mum laugh. A lot. Mum piles pizzas into the oven and I think about how Will loves pizza and I want to just ring him up and break the rules and scream at him for making me have to be best friends with Mavis.

While the pizzas heat, Poppy's friends, having had too much over-excitement and drama mixed with fizzy drinks, chocolate and sugary sweets, are going hyper mad. They are dancing and climbing up the curtains and squealing like miniature pigs.

Hector, of course, has sneakily eaten his own body weight in chewy sweets and is the maddest one of all, and because he is actually a FEARLESS CHILD they don't mind swinging him around the air like those ropes that cowboys have, wrestling him to the ground and tickling him to pieces. I go to help Mum with the food and she is looking flustered.

'Wish I didn't tell your dad he could go to that gig now! Could really do with his help.'

'I'll help you, what can I do?'

'It's all really hot, but thank you . . . I thought I was the lucky one, I said to him, yes, course go out and listen to four blokes screaming with guitars, I'd rather sit here with seven well-behaved children and eat pizza . . . and what happens? Pork gets attacked, you've got a bleeding nose and Hector – who is supposed to be sick, may I remind you – is running around like a lunatic.'

I think back to when I used to be 'sick' just so I could get some Calpol medicine. Those good old days.

'I know. I'll calm them down. Will that help?'

'Actually, yes, just so I can get my head together.'

I think about reading one of my stories to them, but they are all too wild and crazy and I can't imagine them sitting listening to me open up, and if they don't listen properly, I'll take it really personally and hate my writing, won't I? I have a rummage around my room trying to find something to share with them that will calm them down for Mum. And then I see my maths book.

I enter the CHAMBER OF MONSTERS, which is basically what the living room has evolved into. Hector has his bum out and is making it talk in an alien voice and everybody is laughing hysterically. It is more bonkers than monkeys in a zoo and the friend of Poppy's with the cat allergy (completely forgot about that) is covered in hives. I take a deep breath.

'OK, girls . . . and boys!' I start.

'It's OK, you can call me a girl, I practically *am* one.' Timothy smiles so wide and his teeth are sooo shiny you could hear the 'clink' of their sparkle.

'I want to share something with you . . .'

'One of your stories?' Poppy gets excited.

'No.'

'What? Why not? Read the poem you wrote for me.'

'No, no, I want to show you something.'

'What's all that paper for?' the allergic-to-cats-girl asks.

'You'll see.'

Twenty minutes later Mum calls everybody to the kitchen for pizza. The savoury delicious smell of the cheese and bread is soooo delicious.

I am the last of the stampede to make it through to the kitchen. 'Look at Hector,' Mum says admiringly. 'He's so happy to have all these girls here, he is such a big boy now, I can't believe it.' I keep the alien-with-his-bum-out I just had the pleasure of meeting to myself.

Watching them eat the pizza is like watching lions attack a zebra. Will would usually be here now. He would always come over for pizza, or if not I'd always

wrap him up a piece in some foil and give it to him when I saw him next. Not any more. Poppy's mates are all so sleepy now and join Pork and Lamb-Beth on the couch whilst Mum and I tidy up the kitchen together.

'I'm going to get a phone call off that poor girl's mum! She wasn't supposed to go near the cat.'

'Huh?' I pretend I don't know what she means.

'Come on, Darcy, she looks like she's slept with a sieve over her face.'

'They were all playing with Pork. We forgot about her allergy. They wanted him to wear pyjamas!'

'Her mum left me some tablets, just in case.' Mum shuffles about for them. 'Imagine how much the mice would have loved THIS lot!' she says, tidying away the crumbs of pizza from the floor; almost impossible as there is so much it's like sand grains on a beach.

'Lucky we got Pork before the sleepover,' I add, 'or we'd have an infestation.'

'Aw, bless Lamb-Beth, though, she was so terrified for Pork. Kevin is a big dog.'

299

'Pork shouldn't have been in his garden!' I defend Kevin because I love Henrietta, the kindest, most wonderful next-door neighbour.

'Yes . . . that's a point . . .' Mum pauses with her hand on her hip. 'Why was Pork outside in the garden anyway? He's not allowed outside.'

Uh-oh.

Poppy runs in. I could kiss her. Phew.

'Mum, Darcy, can we show you something?'

'Can I just finish cleaning up?'

'Please?' Poppy pulls her baby rabbit eyes out deliberately for Mum to see.

'Fine, come on then.'

But then . . . there's a knock at the door. 'Is this a joke? I'm about to lose my marbles here!' Mum says, looking at me worriedly. 'What if it's Cat Allergy's mum come to tear my hair out before I get her daughter to take her tablets?' she whispers before she goes to open the door.

'It won't be – how would she even know yet?' Secretly I am BATHING IN THIS DRAMA.

'MUM, DARCY! COME ON!' Poppy squeals from the living room. We both ignore her.

'COMING!' Mum shouts to the *stranger* on the other side of the door, as I turn to the living room, only to be quite blown away. Just like Will and I had done the day before in maths, Poppy and all of her friends have designed their ideal houses. Complete with jacuzzis, flowers, jungles, trampolines, ballrooms, dance studios, Japanese gardens, bandstands, circular beds and disco balls – and all of them are so proud, pointing out their favourite bits and describing the exact fabrics and colours and décor. Their faces blush, allergy girl more than most, when they explain how their plans will go, and their voices are excited and so happy.

I can a bit hear Mum at the door being friendly and I think I hear Annie's voice. Mum enters. Annie's perfume hits me before I see her – she smells like how you would want a pop star to smell. Mum walks her in and I feel small and stupid on the couch in my cheeseburger pyjamas.

'Hi, Darcy.'

'Hi, Annie.' I put on an *I don't care you're here* voice but I think it's awfully unconvincing. I suddenly feel really aware of myself, and I don't want to look like I'm playing with little kids in front of Annie. Poppy waves at Annie and gets a bit shy, and Timothy lets his eyes dissect Annie and her outfit like she's on a catwalk.

'Sorry about the . . . everything.' Mum looks embarrassed at the house. 'It's been one of those weeks!'

'Yeah, us too.' She smiles. She looks like Will when she smiles.

Mum says, 'Can I get you something? A glass of wine perhaps?' Mum is always looking for an excuse to crack open a bottle. 'Come through to the kitchen, it's less mad there.'

'I'm driving, but I could murder a cup of tea.' Annie smiles.

'Tea, of course.' Mum's sad, but hides it well – she loves holding a glass of wine in her hand and talking.

'Thanks, Mollie.' Annie tilts her head at me and her eyes go all softy soft on me. I think about why anybody would want to murder a cup of tea. How would you go about murdering boiling hot liquid? Surely every time you went to grasp it, it would leak out through your fingers?

She sits down next to me at the table and I surprise myself but I automatically cuddle her. I don't think we've ever had an emotional actual moment like this, but I can't face Will moving away and leaving me. I cry really hard a bit, and breathe in her hair and her jealousy-creating turtle-neck jumper and the smell of her growed-up moisturizer and hairspray and pop-star perfume. I think she might have also recently had some chewing gum.

'Is that your injury from having a jacket potato

thrown at your face?' she asks.

I nod. 'It was nature's grenade,' I grumble, and relive the sting and I begin to cry.

'Stop it, don't cry.' She strokes my back and hugs me. 'Oi, no crying, OK?'

'Sorry, Annie . . . I just . . . will really miss you and Will so much and I hate crying because it's what babies and stupid girly girls do . . . sorry.' I feel the scab around my nose, it burns and tingles. Mum sniffles a bit. 'I don't think . . . I really don't think I can do this school thing without him.'

'This is what I wanted to talk to you about, so please stop. Stop.' Annie wipes my tears away with her sweet-smelling sleeve.

I sniffle. 'I am just really sad,' I open up, 'but I couldn't say to Will about how sad I was, because I was afraid he would be weird with me and think I a bit loved him and then I wasn't allowed to call and we were in trouble and I HATE Olly and Clementine and then I started to just feel totally cross at him, like so annoyed at him for leaving me. I am MORE annoyed that he didn't tell me in private to warn me, so I wouldn't have to deal with the shock at school and feel weird. Then we might have enjoyed our day and prepared and maybe even had a little party? And now there's no time for a party or even a goodbye – it's just over and I know I won't cope well because I didn't cope even one bit when he wasn't at school for a couple of days so how can I cope for an ever? I'll have to be friends with Mavis the receptionist and Will . . . well, he'll just be a werewolf.'

'DARCY!' Annie finally shouts, and her voice reminds me that I'd been ignoring her the whole time during my stupid speech. I do that a lot.

'Sorry.' I dribble and snot a bit leaks out of my nose mixed a bit with blood.

'Darcy, Will isn't leaving, he isn't going anywhere.'

'WHAT? He's not leaving? He's not going?' My tears dry quick, and a shoot of dribble snots down my top lip. I wipe it away with my sleeve.

'No. Dad came back and tried to make us move in with him, but neither of us wanted to and so we won't be. He has basically got a really good job now, more money, and he feels guilty. As if money could buy us back when we've managed all these years without receiving a penny from him! Anyway, he arrived at school that day, which I didn't know was going to happen, then he picked me up from work. I wouldn't have even got in the car if Will hadn't already been inside it. I couldn't bear the idea of him kidnapping Will and dragging him back to the countryside with all of his brainwashing! Anyway, he took us for lunch, a proper posh one, and said he was going to stay and wouldn't leave until we agreed to go back with him. Obviously he didn't stick around for long! Will and I are more stubborn than he thinks – we have our mum to thank for that.'

I smile, I would like to have met her. 'So why did Will tell me he was moving away?'

Annie looks ashamed of herself and folds her hair behind her ears. 'Well . . . Dad coming and taking us to a posh restaurant for lunch, buying Will loads of presents and treats . . . it annoyed me . . . it was pathetic! As if he could make up for lost time in a few hours of shopping! Of course Will was excited. We don't have the money to do things like that normally. Suddenly here comes *DAD* the superhero out of the woodwork to save the day – he might as well have worn a Superman costume! It seemed like he had undone all the hard work Will and I had done to boot him out of our lives and suddenly living with Dad seemed glamorous, fun and promising and I seemed . . . rubbish.'

'Will loves you, Annie,' I mumble.

'I know that now.' She looks embarrassed again. 'Dad was trying to convince me it was the right decision. I was basically having a custody row with my own dad. Ridiculous. If Mum was still alive she would have been devastated. He bought all these school prospectus things with him from all these new posh schools with big fields and swimming pools. Being all flashy and smug and waving them in our faces, and then he asked to see Will's grades. Which I know haven't been great over the last few months.'

This shocked me, as Will was always a genius in my mind. Annie took a breath.

'It was stupid, but I started to panic. I've tried so hard to do the very best I can for Will, but bringing him up on my own isn't always easy, and with all the drama at home, it just became too much. As you can imagine the school started to worry once they heard about Dad arriving unannounced. They aren't used to big sisters bringing their younger brothers up, and they don't like it very much. It made us seem unhinged. Anyway, we . . . Will and I had a massive fight about his grades and school and *stuff* and that. With the pressure of Dad, I snapped at him and said he was going to live with Dad then, that it was his last day or whatever – which was stupid of me.

Then he went to school and I didn't think he'd take it seriously but he obviously clearly did.'

'So he's not going? He's not leaving? He's staying here, with me?'

'Yes, of course. It was a silly row and I just said it to scare him! Do you really think I'd let Dad turn up after years of not even a birthday card and take my baby brother away from me? I don't think so!'

I leap up in the air and WAAAAAHHOOOO! a bazillion times, and Annie laughs and giggles and jumps up and down and Mum laughs at me dancing and leaping everywhere and I shout, 'IT WAS A TRICK! WILL'S NOT GOING ANYWHERE!'

even though she definitely heard that with her own ears and then she reaches for the wine anyway. Any excuse.

'Where's Will?' I suddenly ask when I get my breath back – that's probably the most exercise I've done in a LONG time.

'Ah, well, firstly you two are banned from seeing each other until Monday . . . so dramatic! Thought I'd let him sweat for a bit – he's got homework to catch up on from the days he missed, so he is trying to show me he can improve and work harder in case there's a chance I won't send him to Dad's.' We laugh, even though it's a bit mean. 'I'm going to stop off and get some food on the way home and bring him some treats and come clean . . . I guess . . . He won't find the joke that funny if I make him stay in the whole weekend! But as you're on the way, I thought I'd drop round and tell you today too. You're his best mate. I feel rotten about the whole thing, Darcy. The silly things we say in arguments, eh?'

*

Not even a slice of time had gone by after Annie had left before Will rings me up cackling. He is so excited. Excited about all the normal things that we do and excited by nothing changing. He is excited by the fact that things are staying the same. Sometimes we just need to have the things we know and love under threat to be able to truly appreciate them, we hold them closest when we fear we might lose them. When really we should hold them close always.

Dear Darcy,

Thank you for my thank-you letter. Perhaps we will write thank-you thank-you thank-you letters for the rest of our days to each other until all we can say is thank you over and over and over. Yes, you are right about the whole 'grandma' name addressing. I tell you what's the oddest thing, going from having a name, like Darcy, to then being called 'MUM' yourself, nothing is more strange than that. Or when your own children grow up to become adults and then their children call your children 'Mum' and 'Dad'. That never gets old.

Yes, I do wish there was more blood in fairy tales, I always got so annoyed when they created these terrifying witches and monsters and evil kings and queens and never told us the gore. I would love to see a REAL fight in a fairy tale, an actual battle! Wouldn't that be fantastic. Perhaps you could write one?

Must go, my cherry buns will burn in the oven – (wink) and for POPPY'S PLEASURE AND CONVENIENCE please find some COINS to share with your brother and sister, it isn't much but enough for some sweeties.

Much love . . . I was going to write my real name but then I decided that actually, my real name is Grandma . . . and I didn't want to spoil the illusion. I remember when I found out that Santa's real name was NICK. I was devastated. NICK? NICK.

Grandma XXX

I CAN'T BELIEVE THAT I have an ACTUAL REAL-LIFE FAIRY-TALE BATTLE STORY TO SHOW GRANDMA! How amazing is that? I can't wait to show her. She better not get her hopes up about being pen-pals or anything . . . but you never know . . . I guess the odd letter here and there wouldn't hurt. I suppose. To show I care.

Hold on. Santa's name is WHAT?

Special Chapter

See – what a week? I told you it was one of *those* weeks. I guess you obviously probably must be wondering how excellent it was when Will was told that he wasn't really having to go and live in the countryside with his dad – you probably must be, if you are a wonderer like me, which you must be if you're reading this, nosy.

Will was never good at talking but he came over on his BMX the very next day. (We weren't going to pass *that* information on to school. Obviously.) He listened to me tell him about EVERYTHING that had gone on. How I thought I needed glasses and was devastated, but then I found out I didn't actually need them and then I was devastated about that. How I was a failed vegetarian, about the mice and the kittens, about Koala Nicola and the school magazine (I have decided to give Olly my wolf story for the next edition – Will thought it was FEARSOME and I could tell he THOUGHT it was about him). I told him all about Clementine and Olly, and how I saw them swapping spit and SNOGGING. About the *Sleeping Beauty* book from my grandma and Pork's arrival and Poppy and Timothy dressing him up and then Pork getting attacked by Henrietta's dog Kevin, Poppy's sleepover and the girl getting the allergic reaction and then how all of her friends made their own mini versions of their future house plans, just like ours.

We laughed and hung out in the living room until the day slipped away, with Lamb-Beth and Pork sleeping next to us. Will told me that he got two new pairs of trainers out of his dad, a computer game, a new hoodie, a skateboard and some money. So it wasn't *all* bad news. I told Will that Olly had been raised by both parents and look at what a nasty vulgar bit of terror he turned out to be. It's not who raises you; it's HOW you are raised. And Will in my eyes is a perfectly raised bake. Speaking of bakes . . .

'Want a biscuit and a cup of tea?' I ask him.

'You really *did* spend a lot of time with Mavis!' Will giggles, and so do I, and we decide to scrap that and do something completely different.

'You know what I've always wanted to invent?' I say.

'What?'

'A cake that when you eat a slice of it all of your pressures and worries float away, and I want to call it the Peace and Quiet Cake.'

'Hahaha! That sounds so good!' Will giggles. 'I could have really done with a slice of that last week when I thought I was leaving! I feel quite all right now, to be honest.'

'But maybe there's no harm in perfecting the recipe so we have it ready for the next one of *those* weeks,' I suggest.

And we frump to the kitchen, leaving Lamb-Beth and Pork snoring away and taking turns to fart.

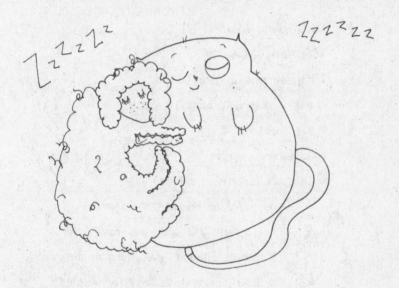

PEACE AND QUIET CAKE

INGREDIENTS

The Peace
Sponge - duh, obviously

200g caster sugar

200g unsalted butter

200g self-raising flour (sifted, or

    else it goes ugly lumpy)

4 eggs, beaten

1 tsp baking powder

1 tbsp milk (cow boobie juice)

A handful of chopped strawberries . . .

    like 6, but you will need more later

    (optional, although everything in life is

    optional, never take that for granted)

1 tsp of vanilla extract

25g white chocolate (BAM!)

The Quiet

Buttercream – scrummy, scrummy, get it in my tummy

150g butter at room temperature

200g icing sugar (sifted)

3 tbsp of strawberry jam (feel free to
  do a dance at this point)

50g white chocolate (grated, not eaten)

5 smashed-to-pieces digestive biscuits

Pink food colouring

METHOD

Please make sure you are accompanied
by a grown-up when making this — you
don't have to share it with them when
it's ready, **OBVIOUSLY**, but ovens are
like *well proper* hot and dangerous fierce
beasts . . . also, I just can't be bothered
to get in trouble and get complaints from
adults that you've burned yourself, so

please just **ASK AN ADULT TO HELP YOU MAKE THIS**. I know you are probably able to use an oven but it will really take the sweetness out of the cake if you are nursing a burned set of fingers.

MAKING THE PEACE

1. Preheat the oven to 180°C/350°F/Gas 4.

2. Grease the bottom and sides of 2 sandwich cake tins with unsalted butter and line the base of each tin with greaseproof paper.

3. You can use a food processor for each stage of your sponge if you have one. We used to have one but now we don't, and so to make sure this recipe doesn't leave you out if you don't have one you can do it by hand as below:

4. Beat the butter and sugar together with a wooden spoon, until very light and fluffy.

5. In a different bowl, beat your 4 eggs. Add the vanilla extract and the milk. Then slowly add this to your butter and sugar mixture. Beat it hard so there are no lumps.

6. Then add your sifted flour.

7. Easy as pie. I mean, cake.

8. Divide the cake mix into the prepared tins and spread it out with a knife or spatula for an even bake. Yum.

9. Lick out the bowl. Oh, and the spoon. DUH.

10. Once in the tins, scatter the strawberries and white chocolate evenly over each cake. Then smooth the mixture over with the spatula so that some of the white chocolate and strawberries are no longer visible.

11. *This is where you need a grown-up to help as you put the cakes in the oven as it involves HOT HOT THINGS.* Bake on a centre shelf for around 20 minutes, or until lightly golden brown and risen.

12. The cakes should spring back when you touch them, but you can check to see if the cake is fully cooked by sticking a skewer or sharp knife into the middle of the sponge (ASK FOR HELP FROM AN ADULT). If it comes out clean the cake's cooked; if cake mix is still on the knife it needs a bit longer.

13. When done, ask a grown-up to help you take them out of the oven and allow the cakes to cool in the tins, then carefully turn them out onto a rack.

MAKING THE QUIET

1. Meanwhile, make your buttercream.

2. Beat your butter until creamy and then add your sifted icing sugar. At this point, add a teaspoon of pink food colouring. If you want the icing pinker, keep adding more but stir in between to get the right colour. *Don't go crazy or your cake will look like a Halloween cake. We don't want that.*

3. Spread 3 generous tablespoons of jam onto one of the bases of the cakes and dollop the buttercream onto the other cake base, then sprinkle your grated chocolate

and crumbly digestive biscuit over both the tops. Imagine you are making edible bunk beds that are about to sit on top of each other . . . and bring the cakes together. SPLAT! Spread more of the icing onto the top of the cake and smooth over with a spatula. Decorate the top of the cake with the remaining strawberries, and if you're feeling up to it, why not try creating some white chocolate curls to make you seem posh.

Eat. Enjoy with a friend. A friend who you love who loves you for you . . . (not in a married way).

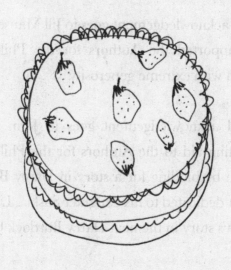

Special Acknowledgements

A special acknowledgement goes to Jill Mansell, who kindly supported the Authors for the Philippines campaign with extreme generosity.

A special acknowledgement goes to John Wraith for donating aid to the Authors for the Philippines campaign by bidding for a story in Darcy Burdock book four dedicated to his daughter Saskia. Look out for Saskia's story in the next Darcy Burdock book!

Acknowledgements

I would like to thank my incredible 'team Darcy' over at the Random Towers. My editor, Lauren Buckland, for encouraging our 'What would Darcy do?' attitude to life and being a fantastic and brave editor, who basically lets me do what I want. Lauren Hyett, for all of her hard work and supply of chocolate fingers, you still continue to be 'siiiiii-iiiiiiiiiicccccccckkkkk' even when you're training for marathons and moving house. Thank you, lovely Harriet Venn, for wearing Darcy Burdock tights and for taking care of us so well. Thanks to Dom Clements for her wonderful eyes and instinct. Thank you to Andrea MacDonald, Annie Eaton, Alex Taylor, Jasmine Joynson and the rest of the Darcy family; for knowing what to do next and throwing me parties and coming to events and all their support. Thank you to Sue for the Darcy copy-edit; I love it when you leave unnecessary comments in my notes like 'I really feel like Marmite on toast right now.'

Thank you to all at WME – Cathryn Summerhayes, Siobhan O'Neill, Laura Bonner, and everybody at their offices in the UK and US.

Thank you to Jodie Hodges, Julian Dickson, Jane Willis and all at United Agents.

Thank you to Becky Thomas for your continued support.

Thank you to Karen Williams.

Thank you to my readers.

Thank you to my family and friends.

Thanks to my beard and husband, Daniel. By the

time this book has released we will have a pug dog called Pig. So thanks to Pig too. Unless he has eaten all my books and then I won't be so thankful.

Oh, and hi so much. My name is Darcy.

I see the extraordinary in the everyday and the wonder in the world around me.

Have you read my extra-large-amounts-of-amazing first and second books?